Needing to do something to bridge the gap that had just formed between them, Michael took swift strides towards her and with one strong grasp, he spun her around and pulled her roughly to him. The intent look in his eyes frightened her more than her own thoughts.

Surprised, Jennifer took a deep, unsteady breath.

"Michael...," she began.

"Yes, Jenny."

His nearness was making her crazy. "I'm worried," she said softly, her heart pounding erratically.

His long hands took Jennifer's face and stroked her cheeks, sending warm shivers through her. "Me too." Before she had time to protest, he leaned down and brushed his lips over hers, deepening the kiss as she struggled against him.

She felt her knees weaken as Michael's tongue traced her soft full lips, then plunged deeper, exploring, tasting, arousing desire. Her heart pounded wildly as she struggled to gain control. "Michael...stop." She pushed Michael away just as someone knocked on the door.

Indigo Sensuous Love Stories

Genesis Press, Inc.
315 Third Avenue North
Columbus, MS 39701

Still the Storm

ISBN: 1-58571-061-X

Manufactured in the United States of America

First Edition

Still the Storm

By Sharon Robinson

Genesis Press, Inc.

In memory of Barry H. Saunders,
who brought so much good into our lives.
Your most important gift to us
was the depth of your love.
We will miss you always...
Sharon and Jesse

One

As the summer sun eased down behind the towering cypress trees, it cast a golden glow that extended for miles. Across the pond weeping willow trees, leaves still green, danced gracefully while a family of Canadian geese patrolled the pond's perimeters.

Jennifer Kelly smiled softly as she looked down from her bedroom window onto the familiar New England scene. Her brownish-gray eyes misted as they drank in the fading serenity. In a few minutes, she reminded herself, her home would begin to fill with guests and the tranquility of the moment would disappear.

With a shiver, Jennifer vividly remembered the argument that shattered her world and her ability to trust. Five years had passed since that day and with time, distance and independence, she'd gained insight and self-confidence, but she was still holding on to the past. Coming home, she told herself, was her first step towards changing all that. Knowing that change meant forgiveness, Jennifer vowed to talk with her parents after the party.

Turning, she glanced over at the clock, then crossed to stand thoughtfully in her walk-in closet contemplating her look for the night's festivities. Feeling daring, she removed her gold metallic pants and matching sheer blouse from their satin hangers and slipped them on over her soft cocoa teddy. She stared at her image in the full-length mirror and smiled, liking the way her recent indulgence fit snuggly around her hips, then flared into a full leg.

Jennifer stepped into gold satin heels that added three inches to her five-feet-seven, and then tamed her trendy outfit with a strand of pearls that dipped dangerously close to her exposed cleavage. She left her thick jet-black curly hair out full and wild.

Satisfied with her look, she descended the stairs to the main level to join in the party being given by her parents for Michael Wingate in support of his U. S. Senate campaign.

Weaving through the crowded living room politely greeting unfamiliar faces, Jennifer's expression brightened when she spotted her best friend's mother. "Mrs. Peterson!"

"Jennifer, how lovely to see you, dear!" Mrs. Peterson exclaimed as they embraced warmly.

"You too, Mrs. Peterson. How have you been?"

"Wonderful." Studying Jennifer, she added, "My, my...you and Brenda have grown into stunning young women!"

"Thanks, Mrs. P."

"So, what do you think of our candidate?"

Jennifer smiled, remembering how her father had raved about Michael Wingate on the way home from the airport. "I'm looking forward to meeting him."

"What do you mean, darling? He's been floating around here for the past hour. How could you have missed him?"

"Oh, I guess we just haven't crossed paths yet."

"Oh. Well, my dear, you're in for a special treat."

"So I've heard. You like him, I gather."

"More than like him, Jennifer. He's exactly what we need for this state. Exactly. Even Jack agrees and you know he's hard to please."

"Then you think he has a chance to win?"

"Don't think—know—he can win. And I plan on helping him do it too. I have plenty of chips to call in around this state."

"Well, this is good to hear. I mean, I find your endorsement reassuring. After all, you've been involved in Connecticut politics ever since Brenda and I were kids. Dad seems to have adopted the man. I can't tell if he's objective enough."

Mrs. Peterson laughed. "Yes. Your dad treats Michael like his son. Actually, the relationship is good for both of them. But enough about Michael Wingate. I want to hear about you. I know how successful you've been in the fundraising field, but your mom's been silent on your private life." Her eyes twinkled. "You know how I like to keep up with you girls. Brenda's dating the loveliest Brit. Oh, I guess she's e-mailed you all about him. How 'bout you, darling? Any marriage prospects?"

"Marriage is the farthest thing from my mind. I've been pretty much focused on work and enjoying my freedom."

"At twenty-five that's what you should be doing. Take your time. How long will you be home?"

"I haven't got any firm plans, actually. But I'll be home for at least the next two weeks."

"Oh, I hope you stay until Brenda gets home. She'll be so disappointed if she misses you by a few days."

"So will I. We'll see. I'll let you know once my plans are clearer."

"Yes, please do. I'll speak to Brenda in the morning and tell her to give you a call so that you can coordinate your schedules."

"Good. I better get going, Mrs. Peterson. I need to find my parents and behave like a proper daughter. You haven't seen them, have you?"

"Your dad's with Michael…somewhere. I haven't seen your mother for a while. I won't keep you any longer, darling. Come by next week. I'll fix you dinner and then we can really catch up."

"I promise." Jennifer leaned over to kiss Mrs. Peterson before weaving her way through the living room and into the den. The usually spacious open rooms made her feel claustrophobic as close to a hundred guests filled the main level of her parents' contemporary house. Meandering down to the lower level, Jennifer paused to check out the videotape of Michael Wingate that was playing on her father's wide screen television. There were a dozen or so people watching the video and chatting at the same time. Her eyes swept the room quickly. Satisfied that her father wasn't amongst the assembled guests, she strolled towards his study.

She stopped just outside of the intricately carved African-mahogany doors. Raised male voices were clearly audible from the other side of the massive doors. When she heard a strange voice utter her name, Jennifer felt compelled to interrupt. She knocked several times, alerting them to her presence. The voices stilled as she opened the doors.

"Dad, the guests are asking for you," she stated from the open doorway as her eyes quickly assessed the scene. Moses Kelly was standing in the middle of the room with his hands perched belligerently on his hips. Her eyes traveled to the back of a taller man facing her father. He turned around. She smiled smoothly at the stranger as their eyes locked. Assuming that he was the much-talked about candidate, she crossed the room and extended her hand in greeting. "I don't think that we've met."

Michael nodded in her direction, then stepped forward and reached for the extended hand. "Michael Logan Wingate."

She regarded him critically, noticing how his eyes, the color of mink, danced with pleasure. "Ah, the candidate. Since we're being so formal, Jennifer Mariah Kelly."

"You say candidate with a hint of condemnation." Michael's eyed sparkled with amusement.

Refusing to back down, Jennifer boldly met his eyes. "I'm afraid you've misread me, Mr. Wingate. Not condemnation exactly...more like suspicion. Politicians have always caused me a bit of consternation."

"So, Miss Kelly, you've been around a lot of politicians? Close-up? I mean..."

As casually as she could manage, Jennifer answered, "Not many. But you must agree that you politicians are generally an unscrupulous bunch."

"Then I'm being judged by the whole and not as an individual?"

"Actually, I don't know you, Mr. Wingate, so I'm withholding my judgement."

Eyebrows arched, he replied, smiling broadly, "That's fair."

"Which brings me to the reason I interrupted you. As I was walking by I thought I heard my name mentioned. And, from the tone of the conversation and the tension I felt when I first entered this room, I'm wondering if I've unknowingly caused a rift between you and my father."

Impressed with her candor, Michael started to respond but Moses cut in. "Michael and I were discussing the campaign. I was telling him about your success raising money for UCLA's capital campaign." Moses hoped that Michael wouldn't tell his daughter that he'd been trying to convince him to hire Jennifer as the campaign's fundraiser without consulting her.

"Thanks for the plug, Dad, but I still don't see how I entered into the conversation." Suspicious, Jennifer turned and directed her question to Michael. "And I'd like to hear what Mr. Wingate has to say." Jennifer spoke with authority, refusing to give in to the magnetism she felt towards the quasi-stranger. When she felt an involuntary shiver race through her body, she quickly looked away, but not before Michael could catch her distressed look.

For a few intense seconds the room was silent. Then he smiled, pleased to see that he was having an impact on her. "I'd be happy to respond. Before you came in, your father and I were discussing the changes in the campaign staff. We've got three months left to this campaign and a couple of million dollars yet to raise. We seem to have worn out our fundraiser."

"I still don't see what that has to do with me." Damn, she thought, looking up at Michael's tall frame, the man's got to be six-five.

"Michael, let's not get into it right now," Moses jumped in, pulling Jennifer's attention back to him.

"Yes, let's. We have a few minutes," Jennifer corrected,

shooting a suspicious look at her father.

With a shrug, Moses gestured towards the armchairs. "Shall we sit?"

While Jennifer settled onto the brown leather couch, Michael and Moses grabbed the remaining armchairs.

"Jennifer, there are some things Michael and I need to work out." Moses spoke first, hoping to placate his strong-willed daughter.

"I'm sure there are, but somehow I feel like I'm involved. And I don't like the feeling," she added defiantly. "What do my credentials have to do with your campaign talk?"

Michael looked over at Moses. Impressed with Jennifer's spirit, he was already rethinking his opposition to her joining the campaign staff. Still, he wasn't going to be dictated to by anyone. "Your father asked me to consider bringing you aboard as our fundraiser."

"Excuse me?"

"Let me finish. We're planning a series of moderate fundraisers in the homes of some of Connecticut's wealthiest families. Your dad's obviously proud of all that you've accomplished in a short time. You know...the UCLA capital campaign and I guess some special events you've coordinated for various groups. Anyway, he just thought you'd be a natural, especially since you're family and a native Fairfield County girl. I wasn't so sure it would work. It's hard to walk into a campaign towards the end...besides, I'd feel more comfortable with an experienced political fundraiser."

Trying to hold back her anger, she directed her response to Michael. "I appreciate my father's vote of confidence, but I'm not looking for a job, Mr. Wingate. So, you can stop trying to figure out a way to get out of this awkward position."

"Jennifer, there's no need to make a hasty decision. Either of you." Moses spoke quickly, thinking that the situation was getting out of control. "I apologize for speaking to Michael before discussing this idea with you. All I'm asking is that you consider working on the campaign."

Hands on hips, mouth agape, Jennifer stared at her father in disbelief. "Dad, I don't think I need to remind you of the purpose of my visit."

"No, you don't but there's no reason why you couldn't help us out while you're here."

"I'm only here for a brief visit. After that, I return to L.A. and that's not up for discussion."

"I'm only talking about three months, Jennifer."

Tossing her mass of curly hair across her shoulders in a gesture of defiance, she glared stubbornly at her father. "Dad, three months is three months out of my life, not yours."

"Jenny, think about it. You grew up here. Know the people. Surely you can give us three months. We need you." *I need you* is what Moses wanted to say, but resisted. "So, what's the rush?"

"Dad, Michael clearly wants to select his own staff—

please don't push." Flustered, Jennifer leaned back in the sofa. She really didn't have a good reason to rush back to L.A. In fact, she had just finished one assignment and hadn't signed up yet for the next one. The flexibility of being a consultant was one of the advantages of not working full time. But the last thing she wanted to do was to work on Michael Wingate's campaign, even if it was a short-term commitment and possibly a good career move. Hoping that she had made her point, Jennifer eyed Michael cautiously.

As their eyes met, Michael smiled, thinking that Jennifer had her mother's quiet, natural beauty and her father's fiery personality. She was also refreshingly candid and surprisingly confident for a young woman. He hated to admit that he'd been wrong to prejudge Jennifer Kelly. While she was more beautiful in person than her pictures revealed, she wasn't the spoiled princess he'd expected to meet. Yes, he thought, Moses was right. His daughter would probably be an asset to the campaign. Convincing her to stay wouldn't be easy, but he was definitely warming to the idea of getting to know Mr. Kelly's daughter better.

Towards that end, Michael leaned forward and addressed Jennifer Kelly with new respect. "Jennifer, I must apologize for how I initially approached your father's suggestion that we bring you onto the team. Now that we've met, I can see that you'd be a good addition. I'm wondering if you'd consider talking this out a bit more?"

Jennifer found Michael's sudden diplomacy irritating.

"I don't think so. I have a life and work in L.A. that I plan on returning to immediately." Knowing that she planned on staying on the East Coast for a couple of weeks, Moses shot his daughter a look of confusion. Jennifer ignored her father's questioning look and added, "Besides, I have nothing to prove. I came tonight just to support my parents."

Michael's eyes narrowed. "If I'm reading you right, you have no personal interest in national politics. Or is it just my campaign?"

Jennifer regarded Michael with impassive coolness and a hint of amusement. "Mr. Wingate, what's so special about your campaign?"

Moses sat back, enjoying the playful sparring between Jennifer and Michael. In fact, he'd counted on a kind of pseudo sibling rivalry to fuel the fires of competition. That way, if they were able to convince Jennifer to stay and work on the campaign, she'd work hard to exceed their goal. And Michael would work even harder to prove that he was worthy of every penny Jennifer helped to raise. Wanting to laugh out loud, Moses held back the expression of hope. He glanced from Jennifer to Michael, noting that his daughter's face was flushed with excitement, and he thought that he recognized laughter in Michael's eyes.

"Nothing, Miss Kelly…" Playing along, Michael suppressed a desire to laugh at her amusing challenge. "At least nothing I can convince you of here in your father's study.

"Besides, you're right, you know."

"Right? How so, Mr. Wingate?"

"About my arrogance." His eyes twinkled with laughter. "I intend on winning, Jennifer—with or without you. And when we do, we'll shake this country up!"

Jennifer's eyes froze on his powerful, commanding body as he shifted towards the edge of the chair and presented her with a silky challenge. "You really don't like politicians, do you, Jennifer?"

"That's correct."

Close now, Michael looked down to study Jennifer's face. "Spend a day with me and then tell me if you feel the same way." His eyebrows arched mischievously.

Taking a deep, steadying breath, Jennifer replied, "I'm not sure I have the time."

"Take the time, please. Tomorrow…let's get an early start…say seven-thirty."

"Early start," Jennifer repeated, realizing that her hesitancy had little to do with Michael the politician. Studying the man, her eyes quickly devoured his handsome face, the cinnamon skin tone, heavy jaw, sensuous mouth, then quickly scanned his rugged athletic body with broad, square shoulders. Sitting taller, she vowed in silence not to let Michael Wingate capture her heart.

"Yes, that way we can have breakfast first before the day gets hectic and I can brief you on the rest of the day."

Jennifer peered over at her father.

Moses nudged her with a slight incline of his head.

Looking back at Michael, she met his eyes boldly and accepted his challenge. "That will be fine."

"Good, I'll pick you up here."

Breathing easier, Moses let out a sigh of relief. "Well then, I believe it's time for us to greet our guests. Are you ready, Michael?"

Pulling his gaze away from Jennifer, Michael smiled broadly at Moses and nodded.

"Jennifer, while Michael and I are winding our way to the living room, you go find your mother. I want us to stand together as a family."

Jennifer inclined her head towards her father in agreement, then rose fluidly from the sofa. Once on the other side of the study doors, she stopped to take in several slow, deep breaths, forcing her racing heart to slow down. Then with a smile disguising her inner turmoil, she waded through the clusters of strange faces, eavesdropping on the chatter about Michael Wingate as she passed, piecing together a picture of a man who enthralled others with his vision and compassion. Now that she'd met the object of their praise, the glowing accounts and forceful pledges of support for him were beginning to make sense.

But she also recognized the raw physical attraction that Michael had stirred in her and wondered if she was attracted to the politician or the man. Shaking her head to clear up the confusion, she reminded herself that she was spinning an unnecessary web. The appeal of the man was what made him such a compelling candidate and also why she was somewhat intrigued by the idea of working on his campaign. No, intrigued wasn't the right word, she corrected herself. She'd never been so thrown off balance by a man before. That fact, she realized with pulse-pounding certainty, would be a complication, should she decide to work on his campaign.

"Jennifer!" A familiar voice rocked through her consciousness. Turning, she found herself facing her next door neighbor whom she hadn't seen in seven years. "Brad!" Jennifer sang out, then practically flew into his outstretched arms. "This is such a wonderful surprise! What are you doing here?"

"It was a last minute decision. I flew in this morning from Chicago. But if I'd known you'd be here, I wouldn't have hesitated." Brad's eyes roved over the slim, wild beauty before him. "Damn girl, you look stunning! Has Michael seen you yet?"

Jennifer laughed happily. "Michael?"

"Yes, Michael Wingate."

"Oh…yes, but I didn't have the same effect on him as I obviously do on you. How do you know him, anyway?"

"We met at Harvard. He was a couple of years ahead of me but he took me on, kinda like a big brother. Anyway, we became good buddies. He's a powerful guy. Don't you agree?"

"Well, I just met him." Jennifer hesitated, remembering the effect he'd had on her. "But yes…he's pretty potent. Look, Brad…I can't talk now. I'm looking for my mother. Have you seen her?"

"Actually, yes. She was headed towards the kitchen

mumbling something about needing more champagne."

"Thanks. I'll try to catch up with you later."

"I'll wait."

"Good. If we miss each other, call me or stop by before you leave, please," Jennifer called back as she continued on her quest to locate Sarah Kelly. She was suddenly very anxious for her mother's calm, easy personality.

"Mom!" Jennifer called just as she disappeared through the kitchen door.

Sarah Kelly spun around at the sound of her daughter's voice. "Oh Jennifer, I was wondering where you were."

"I was...well, Dad asked me to find you. He and Michael are on their way up. They want to start the program."

Seeing her daughter for the first time tonight, Sarah was surprised at the outfit she'd selected for the evening. She's grown up, Sarah mused. "That's quite a chic outfit! What did your father say?"

Blushing, Jennifer smiled coyly. "Nothing. Well, at least nothing about my outfit."

The radiant smile in Jennifer's eyes amused Sarah. It had been a long time since she'd seen her daughter look so happy. Guessing the source of Jennifer's flush, Sarah asked,

"Did you finally meet Michael? What do you think?"

Looking pensive, Jennifer replied, "I'm...I'm not sure. He's handsome, charming, and a bit arrogant. Mom, do you really believe he can be elected to the U.S. Senate? I mean, if this were Atlanta, Georgia, I could see it. But

Connecticut? I doubt seriously if the residents of this state are ready to have a thirty-four-year-old African-American represent them."

"You liked him that much, eh?"

"Mom, this is Fairfield County, one of the wealthiest counties in the country. True, it's the new millenium and we're all hopeful, but do you truly believe it's possible?"

"As a matter of fact, Jenny, I do. I admit that I was skeptical at first myself. But your father had such faith in Michael, I made a point of getting to know him. He's a wonderful, strong, honest man, and a skilled politician. I'm not the only one who's convinced that he can truly be a vehicle for change. Michael's won the endorsement of many of the key newspapers, labor organizations, and women's groups."

Jennifer listened carefully, wanting desperately to find a flaw in Michael Wingate, but she had to admit that she could see how he would appeal to a broad constituency.

"He's Harvard educated, you know—a brilliant, single young man with incredible contacts across the country. Women love him—white, black, Hispanic, Asian—it doesn't matter. They all want to join his camp!"

"Great, so he's a womanizer... that's the last thing this country needs!"

"Oh, Jenny, stop trying to find fault with him! You hardly know the man. Michael's no womanizer!"

"Does he have a steady girlfriend?"

"Not that I know of—at least he's never brought anyone by. I don't know, Jenny. He's so private."

"Let's hope he's not hiding something…"

"I doubt it. If there were something negative out there, his opponent certainly would have dug it up by now. And you know how ruthless the press can be. No, there's been little gossip about Michael. Why the sudden interest?"

"Well," she paused, thinking over the idea, "Dad wants me to consider working on Michael's campaign."

"I see," Sarah replied, studying her daughter and wondering if she would ever forgive them. "Your dad's anxious for you to come back home, Jennifer."

"I know. And someday I will. Not just yet…"

"When, Jenny?"

Seeing the longing in her mother's eyes pained Jennifer. "I'm not sure."

Sarah sighed, not wanting to press further and risk sending Jennifer away again. "Give yourself a chance to get to know Michael. It's so important to your father. Besides, you might be surprised at what you find."

"I agreed to have breakfast with Michael…and to shadow him for a day."

"Oh, that's good. Thanks. I'm sure your father's thrilled. Anyway, we better get out to our guests. You ready?"

"Yes."

Jennifer and Sarah walked into the living room just as Moses and Michael entered to a round of spontaneous applause.

Jennifer stiffened as Michael caught her openly studying him. She acknowledged him with a slight smile, then
watched as he eased his way across the room greeting his
supporters with what appeared to be genuine warmth.

Sarah slipped her arm around her daughter's tense
shoulders and whispered, "Compelling, isn't he?"

Without removing her gaze from Michael, Jennifer
smiled, then answered softly, "Very."

In a matter of a few minutes, Moses and Michael
reached Sarah and Jennifer. Michael glanced quickly down
at Jennifer with a bold and slightly intimidating look, then
turned to face his supporters. Moses' booming voice easily
silenced the crowd. While he had their full attention, he
introduced his wife and daughter, then focused on Michael,
moving out of the way as the candidate stepped forward
into his role. For the next fifteen minutes, Michael's voice,
velvet smooth, commanding, held the group captive as he
shared not only his platform but also his sincere desire to
serve.

Jennifer stood motionless, completely intoxicated by
Michael's message. Unsettling warmth surged through her
as his eyes lingered on her. Feeling vulnerable, she moved
away from her parents, needing to put a safe distance
between herself and Michael. As she leaned against the
wall, Michael, his voice firm, final, said, "I need your support." A shudder ripped through her. As her eyes rose to
meet his, she felt as if he were speaking only to her. "If you
give it to me, I promise I won't disappoint..."

Jennifer heard no more after that. She didn't want to. Sighing softly, she felt her shoulders slump as the tension eased. He's a politician, she repeated in her head as the red flags danced before her eyes. He's a gorgeous, single politician who is probably quietly seducing half the female population in Connecticut. Telling herself to get a grip, Jennifer sensed that it might already be too late.

Two

Waking up the next morning at four, Michael rotated his broad shoulders to ease the ache from another restless night. He figured that since the campaign had begun he'd slept an average of four hours a night. Cluttered long days, restless nights and chronic fatigue had characterized the last six months of his life. Three more months to go, he reminded his weary body. Yawning, Michael sent a burst of energy to his brain.

It was still dark in the master bedroom of his two-bedroom triplex. He leaned over and his thick fingers traced the base of the brass lamp to switch on the soft light. Then he swung his size fourteen feet onto the plush carpet. Shivering as cool air hit him, Michael grabbed his sweat pants and eased them over his naked body.

Returning from his bathroom, he looked down at his persistent erection and remembered his dream about Jennifer. Unfortunately, his hectic, over-committed life left him little time even for sex.

Michael switched on the news and climbed back into his bed, forcing his thoughts from the intriguing woman he'd met the night before. He listened to the early morning news then switched the TV off and jotted down notes for a speech he had to give later that day.

It was during his student government days at Harvard that he'd first tested the political waters and got into the habit of writing his own speeches. By organizing his key points in an outline format, he clarified his thinking on issues and found ways to get his message across to the public.

Gathering his papers, Michael fought the conflicting pulls for his attention: his speech and the insistent throbbing below his waist. Duty won out and he began to write.

Satisfying the members of the Connecticut State Chapter of NOW wasn't going to be easy. He knew that he'd have to be honest and forthcoming on all the key women's issues, like his firm belief in a woman's right to choose whether to maintain or terminate a pregnancy. On that point and the need to strengthen, not dismantle, the affirmative action laws he would not compromise. But his thoughts tended to get a bit cloudy when they delved into education. For example, he could see some value in charter schools, but was clearly opposed to vouchers. Since his conservative Republican opponent, James Thornton, was pro-life and pro-vouchers, the audience, Michael realized, would have no trouble distinguishing between the two candidates.

Michael jotted down deadbeat dad and unfit mother, then leaned back thinking of the confusion, anger and, frustration that these terms provoked in him. Needing some background information, he got back out of bed and headed upstairs to his loft-study that overlooked his bedroom. It took him ten minutes to retrieve the reports he wanted and return to his bed. As he plowed through the material, he eventually found the facts he needed to refute the negativism of the terms.

Fired up, Michael put in details about abuses within the foster care system, the welfare reform movement, and his pet peeve, the injustices of child custody decisions that gave preferential treatment to the mother. He realized that he was hitting on a sensitive point with women, but he also remembered the stories he'd heard during his four-year term as a state representative. Stories of men who had walked away from their children; mothers who had denied their baby's father access to his children. Stories which demonstrated how angry parents and unjust systems used children as pawns. Then he stopped and asked himself what right he had to act as an authority on such a personal and complex issue.

Frustrated, Michael moved away from issues requiring more experience than he possessed and jotted down his position on gun control, education, health care, the rise in bias crimes, racial profiling, social security, Medicare reimbursement for drugs, and economic growth. He went on to endorse the president's proposal to give more tax credits to businesses that invested in the country's poorest areas. He spent some time on the importance of forming strong partnerships, applying his principles to marriage and parenting, as well as to the running of the nation.

Michael stopped to think about partnerships. He'd been as careful choosing the women he dated as he was with selecting his staff. In fact, he reminded himself, he'd been so careful that none of the women he'd dated fit the bill as his lifelong partner. At that moment he'd narrowed the field down to zero, preferring to keep his precious free moments unencumbered by a relationship. It hadn't been a problem—until last night.

He peered over at the clock. In an hour he would be picking Jennifer up so that they could spend the day together. It was going to be a tough one, he thought as he mentally reviewed the day's agenda. But he felt certain that Jennifer could hang in. Breakfast, he noted, would be the only time they'd have to talk privately. If he were going to convince her to stay and work for him, he'd have to work quickly.

Resting back against the pillows, he gave his mind permission to indulge in thoughts of the woman he'd met the night before. He hadn't expected to be so intrigued with Moses Kelly's daughter, but given the enormous respect he had for the two people who raised her, it shouldn't have come as a surprise.

The ringing of the phone broke into his private thoughts, bringing him instantly back into the work mode. Jennifer was forgotten for the moment as he listened to his press secretary lay out the additions to an already over-crowded day. Before he hung up, Michael had agreed to give two phone-in radio interviews and one newspaper feature article interview. He turned the TV back on and listened to more news between showering and dressing.

Finally dressed in colors reflective of fall, Michael turned off the TV just as the reporter wound down a story on a crisis in Ecuador and the threat to overthrow its president. The world with all its problems, he realized, would soon be his to tackle. Buoyed by the notion, Michael felt the weariness evaporate.

Grabbing *The New York Times*, *Stamford Advocate*, *Hartford Courant* and *Wall Street Journal* from his front steps, he climbed into his jet black Nissan Pathfinder and pulled out of the driveway.

At seven-thirty sharp, Michael pulled into the Kelly driveway. He clipped his Star Tex cell phone onto his belt and hopped down from his four-wheel drive, completely unaware that he was being watched from the window in the living room.

Jennifer smiled, happy to see how Michael, dressed in brown pleated slacks, a burnt orange sweater with the top button left open, and brown suede bucks, had exchanged formal corporate attire for the look of a successful entre-preneur. She had to admit that he carried both looks off with elegance.

She watched as his easy, long stride brought him close to her front door. As he rang the bell, she swung the heavy door open. "Right on time." Her eyes twinkled mischie-vously as they raked him over. "I like a man who is punc-tual."

Smiling warmly, Michael's eyes quickly took in Jennifer's outfit, liking her choice of a gold sweater, winter-white tailored skirt and brown suede pumps. "I believe in it. Hungry?"

"Famished."

"Good, I know just the place to take care of that. Are your parents home?"

"No, Dad is on his way into the city and Mom had an early parent conference."

"I just wanted to thank them again for last night."

"They were quite pleased. What about you?"

"It was great. We should net over $100,000." Staring at Jennifer, he added, "So, we're alone..."

"That's right. You're without your allies, Mr. Wingate. But you're invited to dinner tomorrow night. Dad wants to try a new barbecue sauce before he has to give up out-door grilling. Can you make it?"

"Dinner...I'll check my calendar when we get into the car, but I think I'm clear. Are you ready to go?"

"Where to?"

"I have a favorite restaurant. It's a small place over by the beach. Nothing fancy...hardwood floors, French doors leading out to a deck that overlooks a calm bay. The food's good and the place will be practically deserted this time of morning."

"Sounds perfect. I love water and all of its moods." Smiling, she added, "Let me get my scarf and then I'll see what you can do about convincing me you're worth my vote."

"You mean to say there's an ounce of doubt left after my impassioned plea for your support last night?"

"You may have convinced those over fifty, but, my friend, you've a way to go with me yet. Remember that I start with distrust when it comes to politicians.

He chuckled, appreciating the fact that Jennifer had a sense of humor so early in the morning. "Do you consider yourself to be the average voter?"

"No, there's nothing average about me," she corrected. "But as I promised, I'll give you my undivided attention for the next eight hours. After that...well, we'll see."

"Excuse me, Miss Kelly, I almost forgot who I was dealing with. The only thing that still confuses me is your nickname—Sugar Magnolia, isn't it?"

"Who told you?"

"Your father, who is apparently blind where you're concerned. Or am I, the ominous politician, the only one privy to the other side of Jennifer Kelly?"

Annoyed with her father, she asked, "He told you that,

heh? What other secrets did he reveal in my absence?"

"Oh, only that you were caring, stubborn, determined, rambunctious and a bit untamed."

"Um, all that. Well, he's got me pegged, all right."

Jennifer threw Michael a look that tugged at his memory. "Jennifer, have we met before?"

"Not that I can remember. Why?"

"Oh, nothing. It's just a feeling I have that we've run into each other before."

"Six degrees."

"What?"

"You know…six degrees of separation. It's possible that we've been in the same room before even if we weren't formally introduced. But as far as I know, Mr. Wingate, last night was the first time I've cast my eyes on you."

"And what conclusions did you draw?"

Jennifer laughed. "Only first impressions—I promised to withhold conclusions until we've spent the day together."

"Well, let's get on with it…I plan to win you over today. Only then will I feel that I really have a chance of winning this election." Michael smiled broadly. "Let's get out of here."

On the drive to the restaurant, Michael asked Jennifer about her decision to go to UCLA. She listed the things he expected to hear: beautiful campus, warm weather, and diversity of majors. But, she added, something else…distance.

"Why was distance so important?"

Jennifer looked over at Michael, then replied cautiously, "Only child syndrome, I guess."

Michael considered her explanation. He understood the need for some only children to run from overprotective parents but doubted that was the case with Jennifer. Besides, he'd seen the sadness in her eyes. Deciding not to pry, he didn't challenge the simplistic response. "Makes sense."

Pleased that he'd accepted her reason, she asked, "Why? Are you an only child too?"

Michael's smile broadened. "No, I have a younger sister, Susan. She's a third- year med student."

"Medical student, wow," Jennifer exclaimed, impressed by the fact that both Michael and his sister were destined to make a difference. "That's great. Where is she in school?"

"Duke," he answered proudly.

She envied him. "You're close then?"

"Very. We were lucky, I suppose. But honestly, Jennifer, you seem to have reaped the benefits of being an only child. Your confidence and quick wit speak of undivided parental attention."

Unsure if all that was true, she shrugged. "I suppose." A combination of curiosity and the desire to keep Michael the focus of their conversation led her to sit back and enjoy his tales of sibling rivalry.

After studying the menu, they ordered and resumed the conversation. "Why politics, Michael?" Jennifer asked, curious about his decision to run for national office at such an early age.

Comfortable, Michael leaned back and talked honestly. "I wanted to accomplish something…make a difference in people's lives. My dad was heavy into politics so he convinced me to put my desire to serve into organized politics. He died a month after I got elected as Connecticut's youngest state senator."

"I'm sorry, Michael. I didn't know."

"It's all right. I met your father my first year in politics. He and my dad were friends, but I didn't get to really know Moses until after my father passed away. He became my mentor, convincing me to set my sights for Congress. Connecticut was in need of a favorite son for the Democratic Party. The senate seat has traditionally been held by a liberal Democrat. When the incumbent, Joe Connelly, announced his retirement, I slid into the opening. As soon as I announced, there was a fair amount of support for my candidacy right from the start. The rest you know." Michael paused. "I like politics, Jennifer, and I believe that I can make some real impact on this state and the country."

"Is it possible?"

"Oh, you really are suffering from an acute state of skepticism," he mused aloud. "Southern California syndrome. It's definitely time for you to return to your roots," he teased.

Jennifer giggled. "Yeah, well, we'll see. But honestly,

Michael, is it worth the personal sacrifice?"

"Change requires sacrifice."

"When did you realize that you were willing to make the sacrifice...for change, that is."

Michael studied Jennifer. "I breezed through high school at the top of my class, All-American quarterback, near perfect SAT scores, class president, choice of girl-friends...well, you get the picture. I thought I was 'all that,' as they say. I was offered football scholarships and academic scholarships. I chose Harvard because I thought it would open up all kinds of important options. Going to an historically black college never entered my mind...I was going Ivy League all the way. Well, freshman year was a humbling experience. Not only was I not the brightest student any longer, but I was attacked verbally, once by angry white Bostonians who accused me of being one of Harvard's token blacks—a product of affirmative action and not deserving of the place I took up at the University. It was after the 1978 Bakke decision when tensions were still high over racial and ethnic quotas in higher education. While it wasn't the sixties, my friends and I studied the black power movement thoroughly and took to the streets fortified by the words and courageous acts of the militant students who had preceded us. I decided that year to become a lawyer—not because I wanted to fight battles in the courtroom necessarily but because I needed an under-standing of the law to fight in the streets. Am I making any sense?"

Withholding judgement, she simply said, "Go on."

"As we went to war against racism, we took on the larger community. Boston was rampant with racism and segregation. It was the perfect breeding ground for budding revolutionaries. But it was not guns we carried. It was a fundamental belief that we had a right to justice and equality. I led the charge. By my junior year, I'd mellowed—not from complacency but from having won some battles. That same year I was elected class vice president. My senior year, I was president. I dissected the philosophy of Dubois and Martin Luther King, incorporating their vision into my words and actions as I moved from being an undergraduate to grad school at Harvard. My master's thesis from the Kennedy School was based on doctrine according to Dubois. I knew then, Jennifer, that I'd go into politics. With that as my goal, I structured my life accordingly, going to law school, learning all the games necessary to win. No one dared call me inferior after that. And I won't be stopped now..."

As he spoke, she began to feel insignificant. "Listening to you, I feel almost inadequate."

"How so?" Michael asked, uneasy with her statement.

"Well, you found purpose and a mission in college. I found a place to escape. Los Angeles provided the perfect retreat. While there were plenty of political avenues, I was more focused on my classes and having fun. I regret not making better use of my time."

Michael reached across the table and gently lifted

Jennifer's chin. Smiling warmly, he said, "Don't look back, Jennifer. You did what you had to do then. Besides, you'll have even more to offer now. Starting with my campaign." Jennifer's expression remained firm. "I wish it were that easy."

"What's stopping you, Jenny?"

"Past demons, I suppose."

"Anything you care to share?"

"No," Jennifer said quickly. "Well, not right now, at least. But thank you."

"For?"

"Giving me the courage to do what I must do. I came East on a mission, Michael. Listening to you talk reminds me of the promise I made to myself."

"Does that mean we have a chance of keeping you on the East Coast for a while?"

"I didn't say that."

"But if I'm reading your mood correctly, you'll consider it."

Puzzled, she asked, "I thought you were opposed to my joining your staff?"

"Not opposed, Jennifer, cautious. That was before I met you. My staff's tough, dedicated. We work well together. I expect the tension will build to an all-time high as we get closer to election day so I have to be careful about who I bring into the family. I'm sure you understand. The staff's worked too hard to risk disrupting what we've got going. I have a feeling that you'll blend in nicely and add a fresh voice. Oh, don't get me wrong. If you decide to come aboard, it won't be easy to join an established group. There are bound to be some folks who will assume you got the position because of your father's connection to me and to the campaign. But I'm not worried. Your personality and your fire will get them quickly past that point." He paused, wondering if he should press. "Your dad's determined to get you back on the East Coast and I hate to see him disappointed."

Lifting her eyes, Jennifer replied smoothly, "If I come back, Michael, it will be on my own terms."

"Which are?"

Jennifer shook her head. "That's what I came home to find out."

"Can I help?"

"No," she replied, definitively.

Michael nodded. "Okay, I'll back off. As far as joining the campaign is concerned, it's your decision. Besides, it won't work at all if you were to join us for any other reason than a belief that we can win and a burning need to be a part of it all."

As they devoured cheese omelets and whole-wheat toast, Michael took the opportunity to find out more about Jennifer's fundraising experience. In between, they talked about the difference between public and private school education. Since Michael was the product of public schools and Jennifer had attended private schools, they compared notes. In the process, they discovered that in spite of the age difference they had a few friends in common.

As the conversation drifted back to politics, Jennifer's expression turned serious again. "Can you win?" she asked. Michael studied her intently. "I'll win. Enough about me. Tell me something. I understand the attraction of Los Angeles, but from what little I know about you I would have thought it would have worn thin by now. Why do you stay?"

"Ask me that question in January when you're knee deep in snow, freezing temperatures and gale-like winds." Refusing to back down, Michael pushed his point. "Winters make us strong. They remind us to be thankful. Just when we think we'll go mad, spring arrives, rewarding us for surviving the winter blues. Besides, I'd choose a few months of cold weather over the constant threat of earthquakes.

"Well, a minor inconvenience, really," she acknowledged with a laugh. Searching Michael's eyes, she recognized the goodness that lay beneath the surface. "Handsome, charming, and sensitive...my, my. The women must kill themselves trying to please you."

"All right, let's not go there." He wasn't ready to discuss his sex life—or lack thereof. At least not yet. Michael looked at his watch and then back at Jennifer, marveling how in an hour and a half, they'd become friends. He liked her. In fact, he mused, it had been a long time since he'd enjoyed a woman's company so thoroughly. Regardless of what she decided about working on his campaign, he was thankful they had taken the time to get to know each other. "We've got to be going," Michael said reluctantly. He turned and signaled for the waiter at the same time. As if an afterthought, Michael asked, "Jennifer, why are you in a rush to get back to L.A.?"

"It's where I live. Isn't that reason enough?"

"Maybe. Are you working on a project right now?"

"I'm taking a break between assignments. That's the advantage of working as a freelance fundraiser."

"So you don't have an assignment to go back to?"

"I didn't say that. I've been offered a new project. I just haven't signed on yet."

"Doing what?"

"It's an AIDS project. A black-tie affair Hollywood style."

"When do you have to let them know?"

"Soon," Jennifer replied, purposely vague. She'd made no commitments on the West Coast.

"Then there's still a chance," Michael muttered under his breath. "Tell me, does your desire to get back to L.A. have anything to do with a man?"

"No, I'm not dating anyone that seriously. And since you brought up the topic, isn't marriage an asset for political office?"

"It is. The right marriage. I'm selective." His eyes twinkled as his lips curved into a seductive smile.

"Is it the truth?"

"Yes."

"No girlfriend hanging in the wings waiting to step forward as your fiancée?"

"No woman waiting anywhere for me."

"You expect women to believe that a handsome, eligible guy like yourself isn't attached to someone?"

He hesitated for a minute. "I have a few women friends and we hang out occasionally, but that's about it. What about you? Are you sure there isn't someone waiting for you back in L.A.?"

"I'm positive. Like you, I have friends. But no, I wasn't involved with anyone special."

"I can't believe that some man hasn't snagged you yet." Resentful of his phrasing, she repeated it, hoping he heard how ludicrous it sounded. "Snagged?"

"Well, you know what I mean. No hot love affair? No proposals for marriage?"

"I told you that I'm not involved. I'm enjoying my freedom and have no plans on getting married any time soon."

Sensing her resistance, Michael moved on. "Okay. Let's talk about the day we've got ahead."

"Yes. What's on the agenda?"

"I'm speaking at a luncheon for the Fairfield County Chapter of NOW. It should be interesting if you're game."
"Okay. Then what?"

"We'll visit a shelter for battered women, stop by a high school for a voter registration pep talk, go by the office...shall I go on?"

She laughed. "No need. I'm all yours...for today anyway."

"Good. Let's get going. We've got to go over to the office for a meeting."

"Sounds interesting. Michael..."

"Yes, Jennifer?"

"Do you truly believe your voice will be heard? That one man can make a difference?"

His expression turned dead serious. "I'll make a difference, Jennifer."

On the ride to the office, they fell into a comfortable silence. Jennifer felt Michael's gaze and smiled over at him, realizing that she was beginning to trust and respect him. She still had questions about his politics and decided she'd hop on the Internet when she got home to find out Michael's voting record during his four years in the Connecticut legislature. She was also curious about how he was viewed by the media. If she was going to consider selling his candidacy, she needed to understand how he was perceived.

Michael glanced over at Jennifer just in time to see a frown cross her face. He wondered what she was thinking but dared not intrude on her private thoughts. He was happy that the tension between them had eased and that he'd taken time to get beyond her strong exterior and discover her charming vulnerability.

Michael wondered about the hurt that caused her to be

so cautious but was pleased to see that she hadn't been trapped into bitterness. Instead, Jennifer appeared to be a gutsy girl willing to confront her past. Hopeful, Michael turned away and smiled. The campaign had taken its toll on his private life, leaving him little time or desire to date, but he felt certain that if the opportunity presented itself, he'd make time for Jennifer.

They stopped by the office, then proceeded with the rest of the day. Jennifer shadowed Michael, exhilarated by the energy his campaign was generating from a diverse constituency. She'd loved watching him charm the women at the NOW luncheon and then walk into a noisy auditorium and quickly get the students to line up for voter registration. She was nearly brought to tears at a homeless shelter. Michael's expansive compassion for their plight was as genuine as his defense of a woman's right to choose.

It was dark before they made it back to the office and she sat in on a meeting. She smiled graciously when Michael introduced her to his staff as a friend of the campaign. Then he made her feel she was more than just Moses Kelly's daughter as she participated in a campaign fundraising strategy session. Before she knew it, Jennifer was lending her expertise as if she were already a member of the team.

As she said goodbye to Michael an hour later, she thanked him for the day.

"I want to see you again," he said as she reached for the door handle.

Jennifer laughed. "You will, silly. You're coming to dinner tomorrow night."

"I don't mean like that, Jennifer. Go out with me. Dinner. Dancing. I'll take a night off."

"I don't think so," she replied, then opened the door. "See you tomorrow, Michael."

He grabbed her arm. "I'm not used to losing."

"Goodnight, Michael," she said, then stepped out of the car and walked slowly up her front steps, unlocked the door and stepped into a dimly lit foyer. She needed to talk with her parents. See how they were going to react to her plan, and then she'd know what her next moves would be. Closing the front door, she felt a strange sense of letdown. Knees weak from exhaustion, she walked slowly across the marble foyer and stepped down into a living room lit only by the glow of the full moon through the floor-to-ceiling greenhouse windows. Jennifer flopped onto the couch and closed her eyes.

Sarah, thinking that she'd heard her daughter come home, leaned down from the top of the stairs and called out, "Jennifer, is that you?"

Yawning, Jennifer snapped out of her brief catnap and flicked on the lamp next to the couch. "Yes, Mom. It's me."

Sarah Kelly stepped down the stairs garbed in a flow-ing silk caftan. At sixty she was still a strikingly beautiful woman. "I was beginning to get worried. Where have you been all day?"

"Oh, Mom, you just wouldn't believe the day we had." Jennifer stretched and purred like a content kitten. "It was..." She paused, trying to think of a way to describe her day with Michael. "He's just amazing, Mom. Just amazing."

"I can only assume we're talking about Michael Wingate, correct?"

"Mom, he's quick, deeply concerned, and truly compassionate. I watched him dazzle a room full of women, then get the attention of an auditorium full of teenagers! He's just amazing. Oh, I guess I'm repeating myself." She laughed.

"I guess this means you'll be coming home for a while?"

Sitting up straight, Jennifer corrected her mother. "No. I didn't say that. While I'll admit joining Michael's campaign is appealing, I'm not convinced that I want to help staff it."

"Jennifer, what's the real issue?"

"You can't sell what you don't believe in and I don't trust politicians, especially the handsome, charming variety."

"I see." Sarah studied her only child. "Jennifer, I wonder if it's just politicians you don't trust? Or men in general?"

Staring blankly at her mother, Jennifer resisted confirming her observation, then gave in. "A bit of both, I suspect."

Sarah understood. She had vivid memories of the argument that had sent her daughter back to college angry. Jennifer had been a junior at UCLA at the time. She had kept her pledge to stay away from Connecticut, allowing five years to pass. While they'd seen their daughter in L.A., the issue that sent her away was still unsolved. Even worse, it had left deep scars on them all. Yet there was something about Jennifer's attitude that gave Sarah hope. She reached for her daughter's hands, stroking them gently. "Jennifer, give Michael a chance."

Jennifer changed the subject. "How are you, by the way? We've been so busy since I got home we haven't had much time to really talk. How's the new school coming?" "I'm fine and so is work, though support for alternative schools for kids who haven't made it in traditional public schools is marginal. The system still treats them as second class citizens who don't have a right to a second, third or even fourth chance in some cases. But I love the challenge!"

"That's what's important, isn't it, Mom, to really love your work?"

"Yes, my dear child. That's what's important. Jennifer, are you adamant about not working on Michael's campaign? You know it's only for three months."

"I'm probably going to accept an AIDS project, Mom. I'm interested in the area of special events and this would be a good way to get more experience. It's a big job with good support from the Hollywood community."

"When do you need to let them know?"

"In a few weeks. The event is a year off, so there's time."

"Maybe you could postpone the start date by a month or so and stay here to help your father with Michael's campaign temporarily."

"Why me, Mom?"

"Because you're family. We can trust you. We're proud of what you've accomplished, Jennifer. And your father and I want you to come home. Your father thought if he could spend a few months with you...well, he misses you, Jenny. We both do. Do you have any special plans for your visit?"

"Mom, I came home ready to deal with the past."

"What do you mean?" Sarah's voice rose in alarm.

"Just that. It's too late to get into a long discussion tonight. Can we talk more tomorrow?"

Concerned, Sarah nodded and rose. "Yes," she said quietly. "I'm going to bed. We'll talk in the morning." She paused, then looking back at her daughter added, "It's wonderful to have you home."

"Thanks. Night, Mom." As she watched her mother move slowly up the steps, Jennifer eased back onto the couch, concerned about how her mother would take the news that she'd come home to find her sister.

Three

At five-thirty, Jennifer woke after a fitful night. She was more shaken by the anticipated confrontation with her parents than she'd been willing to admit to herself. A wave of anxiety tore at her insides. Sick with the inner struggle, Jennifer hugged her knees tightly to her.

Rocking back and forth, she felt the tensions build as she considered their possible response. Unable to control her anxiety, Jennifer jumped out of bed mumbling to herself, "I need to get out of here." She slipped on her pewter jogging suit, ran downstairs and out the front door, got into her car, and headed to the beach.

As she pulled into the deserted parking lot the sun was just beginning to color the sky. The ocean breeze swooshed through when she opened the car door, reminding her to grab her fleece jacket before she braved the chilly morning.

She shivered as she retrieved the charcoal gray vest from the back seat.

Reaching the sand, Jennifer breathed deeply and let the crisp air fill her lungs. She began a slow jog along the pebbly, deserted shoreline, dodging rippling waves as they cascaded against the beach. Her heart rate quickened, helping to keep her body warm and well-oxygenated as her pace picked up. She clocked her run a mile and a half down the beach before heading back to the point where her jog had begun.

Breathing hard, heart slamming against her ribs, her mind racing as quickly as her pulse, she slowed her pace to an easy tempo. What if her parents rejected her idea? What if her sister didn't want to be found? What if once they met they hated each other? What if the tension from the search destroyed her parents' marriage?

Struggling, Jennifer groaned aloud with renewed concern. Suddenly the risks of bringing her family together seemed insurmountable. Gone was the confidence she'd had that she was doing the right thing. Collapsing on the sand, she lay back, making a pillow out of her jacket.

Closing her eyes, Jennifer forced her thoughts back to the day that the world as she knew it had collapsed. As the cognitive journey began, she reminded herself that she'd come a long way from the angry girl who ran back to L.A. after her mother told her that she had an older half-sister. It had been such a shock she'd left home as angry at her mother for not telling her about the girl sooner as she was at her father for his betrayal. She hadn't even waited to confront her father. Instead, she'd packed and gone back to college while he was out of town.

Until that moment, she'd had little experience with adversity. As an only child, her parents had lavished her with the fruits of an upper middle class suburban life and a healthy dose of love as well. While her mother taught in the local middle school, her father built a successful business conglomerate. He'd started a trucking transport business right out of college and had nurtured it into a national company with offices in L.A., Miami, Chicago and New York. Of course, success had its price. Moses was out of town more than he was home. When he came home, he was still absorbed by the twenty-four hour demands of his work. Long before cell phones, Jennifer observed her father with a telephone attached to his ear almost all the time. But there was something else she also experienced. While he was often abrupt and demanding with others, she remembered him as being a gentle, loving, supportive, and attentive father. Another thing, her mother had seemed content with their life. At least, Jennifer wasn't aware of any tension between her parents until her mother informed her that an affair her father had had early in their marriage had resulted in a love child.

She shook her head, unscrambling the memories. She'd shouted at her mother that she should have kept that twenty-four-year secret to herself. The displaced anger had been completely irrational but she just couldn't accept that her father had lied and cheated.

Jennifer sat up and hugged her knees. Her stomach was clenched tight, just as it had been that day. It took her two years of therapy to move beyond the raw anger and realize that she should not have blamed her mother for telling her about her father's infidelity. As time passed, thoughts of her sister began to haunt her. Many nights, she had lain awake trying to imagine the color of her sister's skin, texture of her hair, quality of her voice and her name. She wondered if she shared her love of the sea and passion for the arts or if she were more inclined towards technology, business or science.

After graduation from UCLA she'd stayed on at the university in the development office, working on a hundred-million-dollar capital campaign. She'd moved up quickly and by year three was in charge of raising money from major donors. As the campaign neared its conclusion, she'd decided that she had to resolve the past and prayed that her sister wouldn't resent the intrusion into her life. She'd come home to find her missing sibling. While she hoped that Moses and Sarah would go along with her plan and was willing to lead the effort herself, she was prepared to go ahead without their blessing.

The night she called home to tell her dad that she wanted to come home her father had said that he was thrilled, but then he'd annoyed her by spending most of the time on the phone talking about Michael Wingate's senatorial campaign. She'd kept her feelings inside and pretended to be interested in the campaign by promising to get home in time for Michael's fundraiser. Then, with exquisite timing, she'd arrived within hours of the party. As it turned out, the party had helped her ease back into her home virtually unnoticed, giving her time to adjust to all that coming home represented.

Jennifer sighed, remembering the pureness of the joy she'd felt when her father wrapped his strong arms around her and welcomed her home. The simplicity of that emotion was now gone. In its place was the prospect of the hard work that would be required of all of them to get to a level of trust again. It would start with the conversation she planned on having with Moses and Sarah before they left for work.

The sun was rising now. She gulped in the harsh air hungrily as the thought of the next eight hours sent chills through her. It wasn't going to be easy on any of them. But there had already been too much sacrifice. Too many destroyed dreams, hurt feelings, lies. It was time to come clean and face the consequences.

Her father would certainly resist the decision to find the child he'd chosen not to acknowledge for all these years. But he'd probably go along with her plan for her sake. While Jennifer feared that the search and, hopefully, the discovery of her sister would cause them all more pain, she believed strongly that it was the right thing to do.

With renewed vigor, Jennifer stood and began to walk

towards her car. She'd talk to her father and mother over breakfast, she decided. It had taken her five years to accept the idea of sharing her father. But now that she had, it was time that she took action to bring her family together. Buoyed by the renewed decision, Jennifer started the car and drove home.

🐱🐱🐱

From the doorway Moses Kelly studied his daughter as she pulled a pan of muffins out of the oven. Jennifer had taken up baking when she was a little girl, loving to test her newest recipe on her father. He hadn't had the pleasure of her baking in years and to him, it was another signal that she was ready to come back into the family fold. His baby, he mused, immeasurably relieved, was finally home. Moses wasn't sure to whom or what he should attribute this change in heart, but he prayed that she was home for good. Moses recalled the night she'd called saying that she was coming home. He knew that he hadn't handled her call well. He'd been so surprised and fearful of blowing the mood that he was afraid to dwell on his happiness at her news. Instead, he'd urged his daughter to arrive in time for Michael's party. After he'd hung up, the regrets hit him. By placing more importance on Michael than on her decision to come home, he'd set up an adversarial relationship between his daughter and Michael.

Then he'd complicated things further with Michael by

insisting that Jennifer be brought in to work on the remainder of his campaign. It was a flagrant violation of the agreed-upon role he was to play in the campaign. As an advisor, Moses had promised that he wouldn't interfere with the daily running of the office. But, damn it, he wanted his daughter to come back home and he thought the campaign just might provide the right carrot. Three months, he hoped, would give him just enough time to win back his daughter's trust and convince her to return to the East Coast.

Ever since she'd walked out over five years ago he'd been consumed by guilt and insecurity. Moses shook his head. He really didn't have a clue how to change things between him and Jennifer or how to regain her respect. It seemed to him that he was always walking a very thin tightrope trying to balance his every word and gesture so that it wouldn't be misinterpreted or give her further reason to be angry with him. Of course, it never worked. Instead, it only added to the strained relationship between them.

He'd worried right up until the moment he saw Jennifer walk off the plane and he'd read the love in his daughter's soft eyes. She'd been home for only twenty-four hours, but it was long enough for Moses to appreciate her growth. As a child she'd been clear-headed and focused and now she seemed to have matured into a strong, independent yet compassionate young woman, which left him hopeful.

Moses stepped into the room, the hardwood floors

creaking slightly under the weight of his two-hundred-and-fifty pound frame.

❧❦❧

Startled, Jennifer turned from the stove where she had just set the pan of a dozen piping hot blueberry muffins to cool. "Daddy, you scared me."

"Deep in thought, eh?"

"I suppose I was."

"Anything you care to share with your old man?"

Frowning, she paused, measuring her words carefully. "Yes, but first come have some of these muffins."

Breathing in the aromas that drifted his way, he headed towards the stove and peered over his daughter's shoulder at the golden brown muffins. He smiled. "My favorite. Thank you, baby." Moses bent down and kissed his daughter tenderly on the cheek. "It's good to have you home." She smiled warmly up at him. "Good to be home, Dad. Want some coffee?"

"That would be great." Moses pulled out one of the carved oak armchairs around the kitchen table, sat down and began flipping through *The New York Times*.

Carrying steaming hot coffee in a tall, bold-yellow mug and a basket of warm muffins, Jennifer maneuvered gingerly around the island that separated the cooking area from the breakfast nook. Setting the mug, plates and basket on the round glass-top table nestled in the sunny alcove, she searched her father's face. "Is Mom coming down soon?"

Moses smiled up at his daughter. "Should be," he mumbled, reaching for a warm muffin. After his first bite, he nodded his approval and returned to reading the paper

Jennifer retrieved the mug of Earl Grey tea she'd left steeping on the marble counter, then joined her father at the table. She wanted to hold off on the discussion until her mother arrived. She sat down across the table from her father and picked on a muffin.

Looking over the edge of *The New York Times*, Moses asked cautiously, "How did your day go with Michael?"

"Good, actually. It was fun to see him move effortless-ly from one constituency group to another…" She paused, remembering. "It was a pretty hectic day."

Jennifer ran the day down for her dad, sparing not a single detail. As she wound down, Moses felt a weight lift-ing off his shoulders. She's hooked! he thought to himself. Nodding, he added, "Every day is hectic. That's part of the allure of working on a political campaign. Each day is dif-ferent, filled with new challenges. There's a great deal to get accomplished in a short time. Did Michael take you by the office?"

"We stopped by for a meeting with Jerry and Maxine. Oh…Michael showed me the office you work out of when you're there." Looking curiously at her father, Jennifer asked, "How much time do you spend there, Dad?"

"Not much, really," he replied. His meetings with

Michael usually occurred away from the campaign head-quarters. Moses preferred to stay in the background, which was part of the reason he wanted Jennifer to work for Michael. He needed a pair of eyes and ears he could trust there on a daily basis as the campaign moved into the final round. "So, what do you have planned for today?"

"I was going to stay around here for a while, then maybe hit some of my favorite spots. Oh, Michael can come to dinner."

"That's good. I'm going to barbecue steaks."

"Do you need anything?"

"No, your mother went by BJ's last night and stocked up in case Hurricane Jasper hits the New England shore." He chuckled and looked over at his daughter again. "You know your mother...always plenty of food. But I was hop-ing you'd make one of your pies."

She laughed. "I could go by the farm and get some fresh apples." Jennifer's mind wandered. She used to make regular trips to Gallagher's Farm with her mother. In the summer, they'd pick strawberries and peaches, enough for shortcake and cobbler. During the Christmas holidays, they'd go to the farm and cut down eight and ten-foot Douglas fir trees and bring them home to trim. But fall was her favorite time to visit the 100-acre family farm to select from ten different types of apples. As a child, she'd climb up a stepladder so she could reach the lower branch-es, pluck off the juicy red and green apples, and taste the fruit. In the process, she'd learned to appreciate the individual merits of the different types of apples. Gradually, she'd learned the names, taste and texture of the apples and how to blend two together to make the most succulent pies. Some apples, she'd discovered, were not good for cooking. August was a bit early for the apples to be ripe but she supposed there'd be a few baskets piled high with red and green beauties. If not she'd get peaches. Smiling contentedly at her childhood memory, Jennifer nodded towards her dad. "Yeah, that will be fine. I haven't baked much lately. It will be fun to see if I still have the touch."

Moses winked over at Jennifer. "Great…steak, salad and apple pie." He finished off the muffin and cup of coffee quietly, then peeked over at his daughter, wondering how long she really intended to stay. "Jennifer, did you get a chance to talk with your mother last night?"

"Some," Jennifer admitted. "We were both tired…" Playing with the remaining third of her muffin, she wondered if she should wait for her mother before sharing her plan. "I wanted to talk with you and mom together, but I guess it's best if we talk first." Jennifer's pained eyes froze on her father's pleading gray eyes. In the past, she'd been able to convince him to go along with most of her ideas. Jennifer hoped today wouldn't prove the exception.

Moses folded the newspaper and his arms. "Talk about what?" he asked, giving his daughter his full attention.

"I've made a decision, Dad, and I want your support."

"Okay," he answered gingerly. "What's on your mind?"

"I've given this a lot of thought, Dad, so please don't think I'm just being callous and not considering how you'll feel about this."

"Go on," Moses urged, trying to second-guess her.

Eyes burning, Jennifer fought to maintain her composure. "I want to find my sister, Dad. I want to find the baby you didn't acknowledge twenty-nine years ago."

As if stung, Moses glared in anger. "How does what you want play into this?" he demanded, angered at his daughter's gall.

Her father's angry reaction spurred Jennifer on. "It's my life too, Dad. I'm not a child any more who needs protection and neither is my sister, whoever she is. Damn it, Dad, it's time we deal as a family with the fact that she exists and has the right to know the other half of her family. She deserves to at least know that we care enough to look for her. She needs to know her father regrets his decision. You do regret it, don't you, Dad?"

Moses couldn't take his eyes off Jennifer. He wanted to shout at his daughter, "Yes, I regret making a baby and then not being responsible for its life." But he held back, trying to calm the agitation and guilt that her words evoked. After all, he'd thought about nothing else for the past five years since Jennifer learned his secret. He was relieved in a way to have it out in the open. It had been a selfish, cold decision to deny the child's existence nearly thirty years ago. Even Sarah had said as much when she first found out about the baby a few years after she was born. He couldn't change the past but at least he could let Jennifer know that he regretted his actions.

"I have many regrets, Jennifer. Not a day has gone by when I haven't wondered what became of the baby I helped create. Yeah, I was selfish but I was also very determined to keep my marriage intact. For me, that meant seeing to it that the child was taken care of financially. That was the least I could do. Beyond that, I trusted that her mother would give her a good home and marry at some point—which she did, Jennifer. I had your mother and, later, you to deal with and I couldn't take the risk of losing you. I was wrong all around. I never wanted to hurt you." Tears filled his eyes. Blinking them back, Moses continued, "Now I think it's too late. Not too late for us, because your mother and you know the depth of my love for you. But too late to ask forgiveness from the one who got shut out of my life so long ago."

Moved by his obvious pain, Jennifer reached over and touched her father's hand with her fingertips. Yes, she'd known her father's love. In fact, he'd been an amazing father to her. But she felt certain that they needed to reach out to her sister even though nearly thirty years had passed. Moses searched his daughter's eyes, looking for signs that she had forgiven him. "Can you ever forgive me, Jennifer?" "I'm trying, Dad. I dread rehashing the pain…and probably finding out more truths… But I feel certain that we need to deal with all the facts before forgiveness can happen. That's why I came home. And that's why I'm begging you to join me in this search."

Moses twisted nervously in his seat. "What if she doesn't want to be found, Jennifer? Have you given any thought to how she's going to feel?"

Annoyed, Jennifer retorted impatiently, "I've thought of nothing else for the past five years!"

"Now, that's an exaggeration…"

Jennifer breathed deeply, regaining her calm. "Obviously I've thought of other things, Dad, but give me some credit. I know you think I'm being selfish…and maybe I am. But I can't help believing that she'd want to know me…you…even Mom."

"Why now, Jenny?" Moses asked, baffled.

Jennifer paused, searching her father's eyes. Then she began to tell him what she'd learned in therapy, how she'd finally accepted that finding her sister held the key to forgiveness and her being able to trust and love again. She kept her eyes glued to her father, needing to see how he was reacting to her words before she pressed further for his support with finding her sister. The "how" was still a mystery to her. Certainly the woman her father had had an affair with had moved away or changed her name. Without Moses, Jennifer couldn't get to first base and she said as much.

"That's good, Jennifer. That you got into therapy, I mean." Moses paused, thoughtful. "But you can't believe that your sister wants to be found after all these years. There's just no evidence of that being important to her.

She hasn't come looking for me. Jennifer, for all I know, she may not even know that her stepfather isn't her biological father. Can you imagine what a shock it would be for her if she's grown up thinking some other man is her real dad?"

"I hadn't thought about that." She paused, thinking over the problem her father had just raised. "If we hired a private investigator couldn't they find out that kind of background without revealing who instigated the search?" "I don't know, Jennifer. We should wait and continue this discussion with your mother. She'll have a better take on this."

"Do you and Mom ever talk about your love child?" she asked, curious.

"When I first told her about the baby, we spent some time in couples therapy. You were just a baby yourself at the time. A few years later, we talked about searching for my daughter but I didn't think it was a good idea. Years went by when neither of us brought up the subject. Then five years ago your mom came home talking about a similar situation she was working through with a student at her school. We argued because she felt we should tell you about my love child. I disagreed. I left the next day for Chicago and your mom decided to tell you herself." He paused, remembering the work it took him and Sarah to get beyond that crisis. "I don't want to cause any more pain, Jennifer."

"I understand, Dad, but finding your daughter might

be the only way we can really be a family again."

Sarah walked in just as Jennifer was finishing her sentence. "What makes you think that, Jennifer?" she asked, pouring herself a cup of coffee and joining her husband and daughter at the table. She had once actually shared Jennifer's view on the subject but hadn't had the strength to move forward on her own. Maybe it was time to take the next step, she thought.

"I'm going on feelings, Mom. I know that's not very scientific but it's the best I've got right now. I came home to find my sister and I need your help."

"Feelings aren't good enough in this case, Jennifer. You're talking about disrupting lives," Sarah reminded her daughter.

"I know, Mom, but lives have already been disrupted." Moses cut in, saying, "Jennifer, this is not a good time."

"Why not, Dad?"

"We're in the middle of a campaign. I don't want my past to become a distraction," Moses offered weakly.

Annoyed, Jennifer started to fight back but Sarah came to a decision and jumped in. "Moses, I don't agree. We've put this off for too long! We discussed finding your daughter years ago and you refused then, for some other reason. No, we can't wait any longer. I want my daughter home and some peace in our family. I don't know if locating your other daughter will bring our family together or not but it might work and I'm willing to try. I've already done some investigating. From what I've learned, the search itself can be therapeutic. What do you say, Moses?"

Jennifer sat back, silent. Her eyes moved from her mother to her father. She held her breath, waiting for her father to respond.

"Looks like I'm outnumbered," Moses mumbled. He stood up and walked over to the stove. Pouring himself another cup of coffee, he considered what his wife and daughter were asking of him. Turning around, he asked, "What if she doesn't want to be found, Sarah?"

"Moses, we're not talking about children anymore. Both of your daughters are adults. I think they can handle the truth."

"I agree, Dad," Jennifer said, nodding.

"Okay. You may be right…and I know you're going to go through with this no matter what I say. I just want to make sure you've considered all sides to this. The lives that will be disrupted…" Seeing his daughter start to protest, Moses raised his hands in utter exasperation. "I know, Jennifer. Your life has already been disrupted…our lives. Your mother and I are anxious to get beyond this so we can get back to being a family. When you went to back L.A. angry and uncommunicative, it nearly tore your mother and me apart. But we've adjusted to your need for space and accepted our part in the forced separation. Now we want you home, Jennifer. We want you back. If finding your sister, at least making the effort to find your sister, will bring you home, then I'm willing to deal with the consequences. Yes, Jennifer, I'll help you."

Tears welled in Jennifer's eyes. Fighting back the emotion, she nodded at her father. They'd been so close.

"Thank you," she managed with her voice close to cracking. She looked at her mother. "Thanks, Mom."

Sarah smiled.

"I'm not sure where to begin, Dad. Do you have any suggestions?"

Pensive now, Moses nodded slowly. "Yes, Jennifer I do. I'll make some calls and see how far I get on my own. If that's not enough, I'll find an investigator. Now, will you do something for me?" he asked.

"What's that?"

"If Michael asks you to work on his campaign, I want you to say yes. We need your help, Jennifer. The other fundraisers don't have your spirit or your gift for bringing people in. They're professionals, all right, but we're planning a series of intimate receptions in homes of some powerful, wealthy people as well as a gala, which I've started to organize. I don't want to leave the management of these events to anyone but you. Can I count on you?"

She turned away, her mind wavering. The thought of working with Michael was intriguing. She'd seen for herself that he was a powerful, attractive man who had a good chance of winning the election. She had to admit that remaining in Connecticut for three months wasn't such a bad idea either. It would give her the time she'd need to see to it that her father followed through on his pledge to find her sister, which was her goal, she reminded herself.

Besides, working on a senatorial campaign would look really good on her résumé. Jennifer smiled at her father. "Michael already asked me to join the campaign. If it comes up again without your prodding, Dad, I'll accept." Suddenly buoyant with relief, Moses smiled broadly. "That's wonderful. Give Michael a chance. He'll ask you." His smile lessened then. He looked over at his wife and then back towards his daughter. "This isn't going to be easy, you know."

Sharing the somber moment, Jennifer nodded. "I know. It hasn't been easy, Dad."

Sarah nodded, "No, it hasn't been easy." She stood and walked over to Moses, kissing him gently, then saying, "I've got to go. See you two tonight."

"Thanks for your support, Mom," Jennifer called out as her mother rushed out of the kitchen.

Moses walked back over to the table and sat down. "Can you ever forgive me, Jenny?"

Jennifer looked up, her eyes confused, sad. "I want to."

"How can I help you get there?"

She hesitated, blinking back the tears. "Agreeing to look for your other daughter is a first step. I'm convinced that once we find her and everything's out in the open, forgiveness will follow."

Encouraged, Moses met her sad eyes. "I hope so, baby. I want you back in my life...like old times."

"I want that too," she admitted, wishing that it was already so. When Jennifer stood, she immediately realized how shaken she was by the discussion with her parents. She grabbed onto the edge of the table and paused long enough to gather strength. She wished that she could fall into her father's strong, welcoming arms but she just wasn't there yet. "I better get going," Jennifer whispered, her voice hoarse with emotion.

Moses stared at his daughter, wondering where this would all end. "Yes, me too. We'll work this out, Jenny."

"I hope so," she replied, her voice stronger now. Jennifer picked up the dishes and turned to cross the burnt orange Mexican tiles. Pausing at the marble-topped island, cups and saucers perched precariously in her hands, she turned back and studied her father, his still broad shoulders. "I'm going out for a while. Do you need anything?" "No," Moses replied without looking up.

꒜꒜꒜

As Moses stacked the charcoal bricks along the base of the grill, he thought about the conversation he'd had with Jennifer and Sarah earlier. Soaking the bricks with lighter fluid, he stood back and watched them burst into flames, reminding him of the potential volatility of locating his other child. But Jennifer was correct. It was past time to face up to his transgressions. It was time to find his other child and attempt to make amends. Child, he hissed, disgusted with his youthful irresponsibility. She was a woman now. A grown woman, he reminded himself.

He eyed the fire cautiously. Deciding against more fluid, he moved to settle in a cushioned chaise longue nearby. His expression clouded in anger. He'd messed up royally and it was past time to make amends to the women in his life. Moses considered his options. He hadn't maintained any contact with his child's mother and hadn't heard even a rumor about her for over twenty-five years. The last he'd heard was that she'd married and moved out of state. Despite what he'd said to Jennifer, he didn't have a clue how to proceed, but as he stretched out, he vowed to give the search and possible reunion top priority. He looked over at the vicious orange-red flames that crackled into the sky and laughed. "Okay," he said aloud. "I'll get it right this time!"

"Dad?" Jennifer called from the sliding glass patio door. "Who're you talking to?"

Moses jerked his head around at the sound of Jennifer's voice. "Nobody," he called back, wondering how long she'd been standing there. "How's the pie coming?"

"Fine. What time is Mom coming home?" Jennifer asked, moving towards her father.

"I just spoke with her. She stopped to get some wine and should be here any minute," Moses replied, voice calm. "Michael will be here soon. I haven't talked with him about my...about my past. I'd like to be the one to tell him. Promise me you won't bring the subject of your sister up during dinner. I'll find the right time to introduce the subject. Okay?" Moses turned back to his charcoal, doctoring it up with his magic tools.

Jennifer cleared her throat. "You mean he has no idea?"

"None...I don't want it to be a distraction either." Moses turned back to face his daughter, his eyes sad, confused. "Michael's father was one of my closest friends. I promised him that I'd help get his son into national politics. At the time we had no idea that we'd get the opportunity so quickly. That's why I've put so much energy into Michael's campaign. We're close to winning, Jennifer, and I don't want to let him down."

"You've made good on that promise," Jennifer soothed.

"Yes and no. If it comes out about my daughter, it could be a media distraction. You know they're looking for anything to hang on the guy. The press will question his judgement for selecting me to lead his campaign, given my own lapse in judgement. I can't risk that..."

"I see." Jennifer mulled over the problem, understanding the scrutiny and judgmental behavior that went along with a high stakes political race. This was only part of the reason she hated politics. There were so many games that had to be played. No one could live up to the impossible standard that voters put on politicians. "Dad, it's Michael's character that has to stand up to the test. Besides, Mom and I can attest to the fact that you've been a wonderful husband and father—to us, anyway. True, you made a major error in judgement but you were really young—I mean, that was thirty years ago and you were what? Twenty-five?" Before he could answer, Jennifer came back with her own answer. "Well, maybe not that young, but still, Dad, let's not jump to conclusions on how this will affect Michael. He's an intelligent, sensitive man. Surely he can figure out a way so it doesn't affect his campaign."

Moses smiled lovingly at his daughter. "I suppose you're right. But for now let's leave revealing all our cards to me, okay?"

"I'm not living with any more secrets, Dad."

"Can we at least get through dinner without a heart-to-heart about my affairs?" Moses pleaded.

"Sounds reasonable," Jennifer agreed half-heartedly. Although she wanted to press her father to find out when he intended on talking with Michael, she was willing to let it rest for now. With a sigh of resignation, she said, "Guess I better go check on the pie."

Jennifer disappeared inside just as Michael appeared from around the corner of the house. A few minutes later, she looked out of the kitchen window into the backyard and saw her father joking with Michael. A pang of jealousy shot through her at how comfortable they looked together. She wondered if she'd ever be that close to her father again. Looking away, she busied herself and didn't even hear her mother walk into the kitchen.

"Jennifer," Sarah called out softly.

"Mom. I didn't hear you come in."

"Where's your father?"

"He and Michael are outside grilling the steaks and talking politics."

Sarah put her hand on her daughter's shoulder. "How are you, Jennifer?"

Jennifer smiled, covering her mother's hand with her own. "I'm okay, Mom. What about you?"

"I've been thinking all day about your plan. I'm not sure that it will have the outcome you want it to have, Jennifer. That frightens me. I don't want to lose you again."

Jennifer turned to face her mother. "You won't lose me, Mom. I just want to give us a chance to be a real family again. That's all."

"You're confident that finding your half-sister will do that?"

"I don't know but I believe that we have to try."

Sarah sighed. "Your father and I are behind you, Jennifer. We'll do whatever is necessary to locate your sister. Once we have more information, we can discuss what steps to take next. Is that fair enough?"

Jennifer's eyes filled with tears. "You don't believe that she wants to be found, do you?"

"I've had students with these issues before. From my experience it could go either way. Some wanted the connection. Others lived only in the present and wanted no contact with the past. Your father had a brief affair, Jennifer. He hardly knew the mother and never saw the baby. That must have left the mother angry. Lord only knows how much of the story and her anger she relayed to her daughter. But let's leave this alone for now. Your dad and Michael will be in soon with the steaks."

Jennifer reached over to hug her mother. "Thanks for your support, Mom."

"Doesn't mean I'm not worried about how this search will affect us, you know," Sarah replied firmly.

Jennifer shared her mother's concerns. She hoped that her parents' marriage was strong enough to withstand the pressure. "I know."

Moving towards the patio door, Sarah called over her shoulder, "I'm going to check on the men."

❈❈❈

Later over dinner, the foursome talked campaign and fundraising strategies. Moses, Michael and Sarah listened intently to Jennifer's fresh approach and intriguing suggestions.

As the dinner conversation wound down, Jennifer and Sarah cleared the table. In their absence Moses and Michael shifted away from fundraising and into the personal. Although he'd planned to wait, Moses suddenly found the opening he needed to confess. As he wove a tale of betrayal and personal failure, his eyes fixed on his young protégé, Moses waited for a response.

Michael sank his head in his hands, listening in silence. As Moses wound down, Michael looked up, eyes stinging, emotions colliding. "Does your telling me now have something to do with Jennifer?"

"Yes. She came home to find her half-sister."

Michael thought about the first time he'd met Jennifer and the way she'd seemed so angry with her father. It was beginning to make sense now. He also remembered her hesitancy when he asked about her desire for distance from her parents. Questions kept forming in his head but all that came out was, "Did my father know about this?"

"No. Why?" Moses asked, not sure where Michael was going with his question.

"I don't know, Moses. I guess I wanted to know how he advised you. I'm at a loss myself. What are you going to do?"

"Look for my other daughter," Moses stated. Just as he started to elaborate, Jennifer stepped back into the dining room, her arms extended in proud offering. She set the warm peach cobbler in the center of the table. Sarah appeared right behind her with dessert dishes and vanilla ice cream.

And Michael froze his thoughts.

Sarah eyed the two men sharply. She knew immediately what they'd interrupted and wondered how Michael had taken the news. When she glanced at her husband he motioned for her to take a seat. Further signaling the abrupt end to their discussion, he looked at Michael and commented, "My daughter's smart, beautiful, talented and a master baker."

Michael whipped his head around to meet Jennifer's gaze. "You baked this?"

She laughed at his surprise. "I did."

"Is the crust from scratch?"

"That's right," Jennifer replied, spooning through the flaky crust with ease. She offered the first bowl of cobbler to her father.

Michael's eyes followed the juicy dessert. "Peach...my favorite," he purred.

"You have my dad to thank. He insisted that I make a run to the apple orchard and pluck a dozen apples off the tree, but it's too early in the season for Connecticut apples." she said, spooning out a generous helping for him. "With or without ice cream?"

Michael chuckled at the image. He remembered his mother taking him apple picking when he was a little boy.

"Definitely with."

"What about you, Dad?"

"Just a small scoop for me."

The room grew silent while they devoured dessert. Then Moses observed, "This is incredible, Jennifer. What a nice treat. And you were worried that you'd lost your touch."

"Jennifer, you're full of surprises," Michael added. "Got that right, Mr. Wingate," she said, winking over at her new friend.

Sarah smiled proudly at her daughter. "Jennifer started cooking when she was six, standing on a chair beside me in the kitchen. But she exceeds my skills when it comes to making pie."

"Okay, you guys, enough praise," Jennifer said, taking her seat and diving into her cobbler.

After he swallowed his last mouthful, Moses looked up at his daughter. "Jennifer, I told Michael about my first-born."

Dropping her fork, Jennifer stared at her father. "I see," she said, quietly turning to face Michael. "I'm sorry that we had to bring you into our well-kept family secret."

"Jennifer, I admit it took me by surprise, but I hope you know that you can trust me."

Sarah spoke first, "Michael, we trust you and consider you family."

Moses nodded in agreement. "That's right, Michael."

"How will you go about looking for your daughter?" Michael asked Moses.

"Jennifer, Sarah and I have agreed to start the search on our own." Moses smiled at his daughter.

Michael glanced over at Jennifer, understanding why she'd been hesitant to tell him about her past. His admiration of her jumped to another level. What a brave, remarkable young woman she must be, he thought. His eyes shifted to Moses. The man whom he'd held in such high esteem since he was twelve, the man who now served as his father figure, mentor, and adviser, was warning him of the role character played in a campaign. Michael paused, measuring his words carefully. "I know this is hard on all of you, but it's wonderful that you've agreed that it is a family problem. I can only imagine the amount of soul searching that went into this decision. How can I be of help?"

Moses waved away his offer. "Thanks, but we're handling it and you have more than enough on your plate."

"This is far from a one-sided relationship. You've been like a father to me over the years. Please don't shut me out now."

Moses coughed away the raw emotion that was momentarily obstructing his voice. "I appreciate your offer of help." Clearing his throat, he said, "I have some idea of how to get some information. I'll take the search as far as I can and then, if necessary, hire a private investigator." He looked at Michael soberly. "If this gets out, it could cause a stir and affect your campaign."

Jennifer suddenly excused herself and headed towards the kitchen.

"Don't worry about the campaign. Just take care of your family," Michael said, his eyes on the kitchen door. Then he came to a decision. "I'm going to ask Jennifer again to stay on and help with my campaign." He looked Moses squarely in the eyes. "I hope to God she agrees."
"Don't do it because you pity her," Moses voiced. "She'll spot it in a minute and resent you like hell."

Michael laughed. "Don't worry. My decision is purely selfish. I need her." He rose and gathered the remaining dishes. "Moses. Sarah. If you'll excuse me..."

FOUR

"ow long can you stay?" Michael asked Jennifer as they finished drying the last of the dishes.

"Until you get elected," she replied, having decided not to wait for him to ask a second time.

Michael couldn't contain his surprise or the pleasure in his voice. "So, you're going to help me after all?"

"I'm going to help us." She felt completely committed to the idea. "We need your voice in the U.S. Senate, Michael, and I'm going to help you get there. Three months—that's all I'm committing to. Do we have a deal?"
"My, my, Miss Kelly, I can't possibly lose with that kind of strength behind me. Yes, it's a deal." Michael extended his hand towards Jennifer and they sealed the deal with a firm handshake.

"Good, then you'll have my undivided attention with the exception of the search for my sister. I'm going to help with that, you know."

"Yes, I know. I'm behind you one hundred percent."

Jennifer looked hard at Michael. "Aren't you worried about the impact my father's revelations could have on your campaign?"

Michael returned her gaze. "Not really. Besides, I'm gaining confidence that I'll survive whatever storm lies ahead. By the way, when can you start working on the campaign?"

"Immediately," she answered without reservation.

Michael smiled. "Good. Then let's head to the office."

She laughed. "Well, I guess I asked for that. Okay," Jennifer said over her shoulder as she headed upstairs to get her jacket and say goodbye to her mother.

Michael headed to Moses' study. A few minutes later when Jennifer found the two friends, they were totally absorbed in a Yankee/Cleveland baseball game. Each team was fighting for the division lead as the season neared its end. Jennifer stood at the door and signaled Michael that she was ready to leave. They said goodnight to Moses and he distractedly acknowledged their departure.

"You a baseball fan?" Jennifer asked Michael as he held the car door open for her.

"Too slow for me…I'm into the hoops, mostly waiting for my Knicks to bring me home another trophy. With or without Patrick, we'll get them this year." Michael closed her door and went around to climb into the driver's seat.

Jennifer laughed.

"What about you? Are you a fan?" The car hummed quietly as he threw it into drive and eased onto the windy, narrow streets.

"Yeah, Dad started taking me to Sunday afternoon games when I was four. He's a Mets season ticket holder to this day. Got box seats right along the third base line. He loves watching the players tear around the third base line determined to make it home safely." She chuckled, remembering the first time she caught a fly ball. "When I was a kid, I used to go with him to games prepared to catch a ball with my mitt. One day it paid off. A foul ball ricocheted off the seat a few rows in front of me, then bounced up into my eagerly positioned mitt. My dad had to block a few people to make sure I wasn't knocked down in the process. We laughed hysterically afterwards. Dad worked some magic and got the whole team to sign that ball. I always figured that he told the manager some hard luck story about his only daughter and won over the guy's sympathy." She chuckled. "Anyway, it's still on the bookcase in my bedroom."

"You and Moses are pretty close, I gather."

"Were close," she replied.

Michael peeked over at Jennifer. He could only imagine what damage had been done when she found out about Moses' other daughter. "Look, Jennifer, let's forgo the office for now. I have a quiet spot that we could go to and talk in private."

She frowned at Michael. "I thought you wanted to go to the office?"

"I will later. Right now I want to talk about you."

She laughed loudly. "Now, Mr. Wingate, all you really need to know about me is how well I can raise money, right?"

Michael considered her question, not ready to reveal how deep his interest in her went. "Yes and no. Hear me out on this, Jennifer...I mean, raising money is your job but we need to know each other quickly to be successful. Do you agree?"

"I suppose..."

"Starting tomorrow you'll be thrown into our hectic twelve to fourteen hour days. So, we better take advantage of this quiet evening." Michael winked at Jennifer, hoping he'd convinced her that his interest in her was professionally motivated.

Jennifer mulled over the idea in her head. If they went to the office, she could jump into the work and be distracted from her worries. On the other hand, Michael was right. She knew too little about the man she'd just committed to selling. Taking some time to get to know him would be helpful.

Michael watched Jennifer in silence, noticing that she was putting too much thought into what he considered a natural phase in the process.

"Oh come on, Jennifer, it's really not all that threatening. We can take this work thing a bit slower. Tomorrow morning is soon enough. Tonight I'd like to just talk a while. Okay?"

"I guess," she agreed, then turned to stare out the window. Truth was, she was exhausted emotionally and not ready to share her problems with anyone, much less the man who was now her boss. On the other hand, she could use a quiet detour before jumping into the intensity of the campaign.

Michael deftly veered his truck into the far right lane and exited the highway. He figured to spend some time with Jennifer, drop her off and then head over to his office and work for a few hours. Or maybe he'd give Jennifer the option of going with him to the office. First, he wanted to build her trust in him. Michael clicked on his CD player, allowing the melodic Sade to dictate the mood for the moment.

As he drove, Michael sent Jennifer into stitches talking about his fan club that included two feisty sisters, Mildred and Maxine, whom he suspected to be nearing eighty. He described how they showed up at all his events dressed in pink and purple flowered dresses with ornate, wide-brimmed hats. He'd been so enchanted with the sisters that he'd finally given in to their repeated request that he visit them in their home in Lyme. Jennifer stopped laughing when Michael reported that his trip over the Connecticut River had netted him their absolute loyalty and a campaign pledge of a quarter of a million dollars. Since that fruitful visit, he'd made numerous trips to the wealthy New England town for parties given by the sisters. He'd discovered that underneath their eccentricity were two staunch Democrats well positioned within the wealthy waterfront community.

Jennifer matched Michael's story with one from her work on the UCLA capital campaign. Only hers was a tale of a former Hollywood actress whose current boy toy was a UCLA graduate who wanted her to help boost his stature within the university. She'd invited Jennifer to tea and handed her a metal box. She was instructed not to open it until she returned to her office. Jennifer had been blown away when she counted her take—twenty-five thousand in hundred-dollar bills as a first installment for a gift in her boyfriend's name. The actress ultimately funded a chair in the School of Drama in his honor.

Michael pulled into a parking lot and shut the car off. "Ready?"

She looked at the surroundings curiously and nodded.

He led her into a small bar. The host welcomed Michael and showed them to a secluded booth with a small, rose-colored halogen light dangling from the ceiling. They each ordered wine, sipping slowly as they settled in.

Finally, Michael broke the silence by talking a bit about his vision for the remainder of the campaign. He described the phase leading up to the primaries that he was certain to win, and then the ad campaign that would begin just after Labor Day.

As he spoke, Jennifer mentally calculated the millions needed to achieve his objectives, then listened attentively as Michael filled her in on the team. He painted a vivid picture of the personalities, years of political experience, dedication and even burnout level of each member. He also told her about the consulting agencies for PR and special events that they'd been using since the campaign began.

Jennifer fought excitement. She was ready to get back to work and the campaign sounded challenging. Her mood changed when Michael started talking about Moses. It was clear that the two men had deep respect for each other but she wondered why his opinion of her father hadn't shifted at all, given what he'd just learned about his secret past. His next question made her think he'd been reading her mind.

"Jenny, I'm sure the news about your half-sister hit you pretty hard when you first heard about it. Is that why you stayed away from home for five years?"

Jennifer shrugged. "I guess," she offered reluctantly, not willing to show her entire hand just yet. She looked away. If they were going to be working together, she didn't want him to feel that her personal issues were going to get in the way of performance.

Michael pressed her. "How are you managing now?" She studied him for a moment. "Well enough. You don't need to get involved, Michael. In fact, it's probably best that you stay clean. That way if it ever comes up, you can act truly surprised."

"That's not an option, Jennifer. Your parents are a significant part of my life and they're hurting. Your pain is written all over your face. So, I'm involved. Don't try to keep me out."

Jennifer fended off tears.

Michael reached over and stroked her hand. "Jenny, it's okay."

Touched by his tenderness, she took a few calming deep breaths and steadied her emotions. "I'm sorry, Michael. I didn't mean to do that," she whispered.

He smiled in encouragement. "Don't apologize, Jennifer. Talk to me."

"I'm just so worried. Did I do the right thing? To press the point to find her, I mean."

"Yes, you did the right thing. Moses and Sarah will be fine. And your father needs to do what he should have done thirty years ago."

"I hope you're not too angry with him. He's had enough anger from me to last a lifetime...not to mention what's in store for him from his firstborn." She paused, startled. "I've never said that aloud. I'm not even my father's first child."

"No, but you'll always be his favorite," Michael reminded her.

"Thanks." She peered intently at Michael. "I'm worried about my parents, Michael."

Stroking Jennifer's cold fingers, Michael finally spoke. "Don't be. Sarah's strong and she's also been a champion for kids for many years. I have faith that she'll stand up through this ordeal."

"You've spent more time around my parents than I have lately. How do they seem to you?"

Michael paused, thinking over the subtle signs of strain he'd observed in the two over the past five years. "Now that you mention it, I have noticed a strain between them but I've never doubted their commitment to each other."

"This could break them apart."

"Or bring them closer," Michael offered. "Did you see your parents at all during the five years you were away?"

"I saw them," she said flatly. "I was a junior when I found out about my half sister. I left Connecticut angry. Dad came out to L.A. several times a year on business. I saw him but we steered clear of the subject of his love child. Holding back only added to the strain between us. My mother didn't come out until my graduation. I guess she was going through her own period of anger. Anyway, when she finally came out, she stayed with me for a couple of weeks. She was worried about me holding on to my anger..."

"I can imagine," he said softly. "Did you try therapy?"

"I spent two years in therapy."

"Did it help?"

"I guess so. I'm home, aren't I? Most of the anger's gone. Now I want it all resolved."

"He'll find her, you know."

"Yes, I suppose he will. And then?"

"There's no telling. First steps, first."

"Yes, first steps. Sorry to burden you with all this, Michael."

"It's no burden. You can talk with me anytime you want."

"I may take you up on that offer. I feel a little guilty about rushing my parents into this so soon after I got home. I don't know, Michael, I was just so determined not to let another day pass."

"Well," Michael paused, thinking out his words carefully, "I'm sorry, Jennifer, but I have to ask. Have you given any thought to the fact that your sister might not want to be found?"

"You sound like my dad. Yes, I have, but I don't believe that's possible. And she's got to be wondering about her biological father and the other part of her family. Once we've located her and get word to her that we want to meet her, I think I'll be satisfied with whatever she decides. Maybe my motives are selfish, but I think my parents just need my push. You know how they are always reaching out to the underdog. Deep down surely they want to get the word out that they care about the girl, too."

"Yes, maybe. Sarah's certainly dedicated to working with young people. Just look at what she's accomplished with the charter school." He paused again, not wanting to push too far.

Jennifer pulled her hands away and took a sip of her wine. The pianist was taking a break. The voice of Lauren

Hill filtered softly throughout the club as the CD player kicked in. Suddenly weary of the whole subject, Jennifer signaled the end of the discussion. "Let's get out of here."

"Where do you want to go?" Michael asked, waving to the waiter.

"I think our original destination was your office. Let's go there. I want to get started. How much money did you say we need to raise between now and November 1?"

"A mere three million. A no-brainer for a seasoned fundraiser like you, right?"

"You got that right, Mr. Wingate. In fact, we might just go over our goal."

"I like your attitude, Ms. Kelly. I'm sure the rest of the team will as well. Yes, let's get out of here. We've got plenty of work ahead of us."

✿❀✿

Michael called Jennifer and arranged to pick her up the next morning at six a.m. They had meetings in Hartford and then he planned to take the afternoon off. He put the phone back on its cradle. In the four weeks since she'd joined the campaign, they'd managed to have a late dinner together three or four nights a week. He'd grown dependent on her company and her refreshing attitude towards politics.

He was about to call Jerry when the phone rang.

"Michael, this is Daphne Wade."

He was surprised to hear her voice since they hadn't spoken to each other in over a year.

The conversation started off cautiously but soon they were bantering away in a tone typical of old friends who hadn't talked in a while. They even laughed about a mutual friend who had quit working on Wall Street and moved to the Caribbean to teach school.

Then Daphne dropped the bomb.

"Michael, I called for a reason."

"Okay." He half expected her to ask him for a favor.

"I wish it didn't have to be like this."

"What are you talking about?" he asked, confused, inpatient.

"My parents insisted that I call you. Said you deserved to know. If it was up to me, I'd wait...until after the election."

"Daphne, what are you talking about?"

"Max, I'm talking about my son—our son—Max. He's three months old."

"Wait, wait...you've lost me."

"Michael, I know I should have called you when I found out that I was pregnant but I thought I could do it alone, especially since it wasn't something we'd planned."

After a moment of silence, Daphne asked, "Michael, are you there?"

Trying to make sense out of the wild accusation, he stammered, "How, when?"

"The *Time Magazine* party celebrating a year in review.

My photos were on display..."

She reminded him with just enough details to jog his memory. Party. Yes, he remembered. He'd been so happy to see her. They'd left the party together and yes, had had sex. It hadn't been the first time either and like the other times, it had been spontaneous, without commitment. Not once had either of them spoken of love, but he vaguely remembered talk of birth control.

"But you were on the pill or something..."

"I'd been on Depo...it doesn't matter, Michael. I got pregnant!"

"It does matter. Damn, Daphne," he replied angrily. "How do you know it's my baby?" he questioned.

"I know, Michael. Believe me. I know."

"You don't know anything!" Michael shouted, slamming the phone down angrily. Feelings of anger, betrayal, and frustration assaulted him, followed by denial. Daphne was wrong. She'd told him a lie. Maybe, she'd even been bought off by his opponent.

For the next two hours Michael stayed up struggling with the weight of Daphne's revelation. Even if it wasn't true, he needed to warn Moses and Jennifer. He glanced over at the clock. It was two-thirty in the morning. Too late to call either of them. Besides, he would be seeing Jennifer in a few hours. He could tell her then about the call. No, Michael thought, he needed to talk with Moses first. Get his advice. He couldn't believe the irony. A month ago he'd learned that Moses had fathered a child out of wedlock. Now he needed advice on how to deal with the same crisis in his life. What would Moses say?

As Michael climbed into bed, he wondered, Why now when I can least afford to deal with such a crisis?

Since it was six a.m. on a Sunday morning, Michael didn't dare ring the Kellys' doorbell. Instead, he waited for Jennifer in his car as they'd planned. On his way over to her house, he'd stopped and picked up some breakfast for her. He knew she'd be surprised.

The past week Jennifer had made several comments about his short temper. She'd gone so far as to suggest that he take some time off. To accentuate her point, she'd dropped off a brochure describing a half-day spa retreat for busy executives. While he'd grumbled at the time, he took her advice to heart and he'd planned a quiet afternoon for them away from the campaign pressures.

Campaign pressures. He nearly laughed out loud. He hadn't known what pressure was until now. His life had taken a sudden turn towards disaster. And what was he doing about it? Follow through with earlier plans to take Jennifer to Ron Becker's farm to go horseback riding. However, their hosts, Ron and Nancy Becker, wouldn't be joining them until after they returned from their ride, and it occurred to him he'd have plenty of time to tell Jennifer about Daphne's call.

Michael's thoughts switched to Moses. After all, he'd met Ron through Moses. Ron had become one of his major donors. When he'd maxed out on their personal contributions, Ron had solicited from his friends and business associates. The Hartford gala had been his idea as well. He'd promised to deliver over a million dollars to help pay for TV ads. He wondered if Ron would be so generous if Daphne's call proved to be true.

Michael was in the midst of a mental debate over whether to tell Jennifer about the call before he spoke with Moses when he spotted her stepping out of her front door looking stunning.

Michael's smile brightened as she opened the passenger-side car door and eased into the seat. "Good morning," Michael greeted Jennifer cheerfully, masking his real concerns.

She smiled. "Aren't you in a good mood?"

Without removing his eyes from hers, he nodded. "You have a lot to do with my mood. Here," he said, handing her a bag containing a carrot muffin and hot coffee, deciding that he wouldn't bring up the call today.

"For me?" she said, her eyes twinkling with delight at the surprise gesture. Peeking into the bag she added, "Thoughtful, too."

"Yeah, well, it's to make up for my recent bad temper."

Laughing, Jennifer winked at Michael and dug into the bag for her muffin. "Hey, it's not me you have to appease. I'm the new guy on the team and you've been pretty easy on me."

He smiled. "That's a relief. I thought I'd blown it with you too."

She shot him an assessing look. "No. But I wouldn't mind knowing what's got you so tense," she said, biting into her muffin.

Michael drove out of the driveway without responding.

Sipping her coffee, and devouring the treat, Jennifer continued her analysis. "You're way ahead in the polls and drawing incredibly good numbers at each of your appearances. The money's rolling in. Staff's working well as a team. The media's friendly. I mean…things are looking good. So what's got you so edgy?"

Michael flashed Jennifer a look of concern, knowing that even though she was talking about the campaign, she'd given him the perfect opening to tell her about Daphne's call. But something stopped him. "Guess I need a break. Which reminds me. Did you bring a change of clothes?" he said, redirecting the conversation into safer areas.

"Right here." She held up her overstuffed backpack. "You said dress down so I brought jeans and a sweatshirt."

"That's perfect. And shoes?"

"Oh, I threw in a pair of all terrain boots. Where are we going anyway?"

He laughed. "Just leave it to me. Okay?"

"That's asking for a lot of trust, Senator. How 'bout a clue?"

"Rolling hills, New England foliage, sore thighs," he

said playfully.

Jennifer laughed. "What do sore thighs have to do with leaves turning?"

"Everything," he replied, holding back clarifying details.

"Okay. I get the point," she smirked. "You want to surprise me. Tell me something, Michael."

"What's that?"

"What do you do to relax?"

"Is that a slick way to get me to tell you where we're going this afternoon?"

"No. I'm serious. I've seen you mostly in high gear. I was just wondering what you like to do when you're not working."

Michael paused. "It's been a long time since I've had down time. You once asked me about the personal sacrifice that's exacted from the politician—well, it's a real challenge finding time for yourself when you're a public figure. I suppose that's part of why I haven't gotten married. I chose this life and until now I haven't been willing to inflict its constant demands on someone I love."

"Wow," she replied, shocked by his honesty. "But you deserve more, Michael."

"I agree and I'm beginning to accept the fact that I might need help striking that balance. Take today. I don't think I would have taken this afternoon off if you hadn't gently pressed me."

She smiled warmly. "Well, then. Let's get our work

over quickly so we can escape. Where is it we're going again?"

He chuckled. "Nice try. We're escaping into the hills and that's all I'm telling you for now."

"All right. I give up. I can wait. Let's talk about our meeting then. If Ron Becker has hired a firm to pull together this Hartford gala, what is my role?"

Michael filled Jennifer in on everything about the proposed event and together they devised a plan to support the Hartford team. By the time they reached Hartford, she was prepared for the meeting and looking forward to getting away after Michael spoke at a local church service. By twelve-thirty, they were back in Michael's truck and headed east on Route Two. Michael's mood had shifted again. She admired the ease with which he discarded the role of politician. While they joked about how cleverly Michael had gotten out of the church luncheon, Jennifer was acutely aware that he was serious about taking more control over his personal life.

She studied her surroundings as they exited the highway and wound along country roads. White fencing lined a private road on both sides. Michael turned left into a driveway. Jennifer's eyes grew big as she spotted meadows dotted with grazing horses. "A horse farm!" she exclaimed, and her mind began to piece together the picture. "Rolling hills, New England foliage, sore muscles…horseback riding! But I thought you didn't ride?"

"I've ridden horses, Jennifer. I just never got into it like you did. The farm belongs to Ron and Nancy Becker. They arranged for us to ride a pair of his most spirited horses. They'll be home later so you'll get a chance to meet them."

Jennifer stared at him in disbelief. "You did this for me?"

"I did it for both of us," he corrected, smiling warmly in her direction.

"I'm touched, Michael."

"I wanted to find a way to spend a relaxing afternoon with you doing something you'd enjoy."

"Thank you." For a second time that day she was moved by his thoughtfulness.

"You're welcome. Ron tells me that the views from the hills over there are breathtaking."

Jennifer looked over at the beautiful red, yellow and green hills behind them. "It's been a long time since I've seen fall foliage," she said, touching Michael's hand as it rested on the gearshift. "I've missed this…"

He looked over and caught the longing in her eyes. Jennifer was more ready to come home than she was willing to admit, he thought. They pulled up in front of a rambling stone home and were greeted by the housekeeper, who showed them to separate bedrooms so that they could change. By the time they wandered into the stables the horses were saddled and a picnic lunch dangled inside a saddlebag.

They rode side by side, comparing lifestyles and

dreams. Jennifer probed Michael deeper about his long-term plans, learning that he intended to commit to two terms in the Senate. After that he wanted to go into business. She admitted that she wanted to be a wife and mother someday. She was open to the type of man she would marry, saying that she'd recognize the man when he appeared in her life.

Michael stayed silent on the issue of marriage and kids except to say that he wouldn't be pressured into a relationship. Jennifer picked up a hardness in his tone that made her wonder how many women had tried to push him into marriage.

As the trail narrowed, he took the lead. She followed several feet behind him. They were each lost in their private thoughts. At a clearing towards the top of the hill, they stopped for lunch and eased back into conversation. Jennifer talked about her childhood, exposing a deep love for her parents that was devoid of any signs of lasting anger or disappointment. Michael recalled a childhood that embraced service as an expectation. His mother and sister had partnered on a ten-year community development project in one of the poorer communities in southern Connecticut, while Michael had volunteered after school at the local boys and girls club. By the time he was a sophomore in high school, he'd branched out and started a mentoring program in which high school students assisted kids from junior high with the transition to high school.

Jennifer encouraged Michael to talk about his father

but noticed his discomfort with his memories. He spent most of the time explaining the fierce competition between him and his father. Michael suggested that his over-ambition stemmed from his dad's high expectations and demands for perfection.

As the light shifted and the sun dipped over to the other side of the hill, the yellow, red and green blended into a canvas of muted colors. The horses knew their way home, and their pace accelerated the closer they got to food and water. Jennifer laughed out loud as her horse broke into a gallop when they reached the flat area. Michael delighted in her free, easy spirit. By the time he caught up with her, they were within yards of the stable. He pulled up beside her and they rode the last leg together.

After cocktails and campaign chatter with Ron and Nancy, they thanked their hosts and drove back to Norwalk. It was a perfect day, unspoiled by the dangers that lurked in the corner.

Five

Jennifer quickened her step as she approached the building that housed Michael's campaign office. After seven weeks of working on his campaign, she had not only become passionate about electoral politics but had also come to trust the candidate implicitly. Michael had won the primaries and had taken a commanding twelve-point lead over his opponent as they headed into the final five weeks of the campaign. His success made Jennifer's job easy and she anticipated exceeding the goal they'd set when she took the job.

She had never worked so hard, nor been so happy.

Since their afternoon horseback ride, she and Michael had become very close. Several times, they'd gone out for a late night dinner. Once he'd even taken her dancing.

Though obviously attracted to her, he'd never crossed the line, which suited her just fine. He was handsome, charming, compassionate—everything she desired in a man. Except that he was her boss. And as long as that condition existed...

Jennifer shook her head to clear her thoughts as the elevator door opened on Michael's headquarters floor. She stepped off and spoke briefly to the receptionist. The sound of muffled voices and the ringing of telephones caused her pulse to quicken. Smiling, she looked around at the six people, four men and two women, who were busy on the phones responding to requests for Michael's appearance; coordinating get-out-the vote activities, explaining position papers, making promises, and cutting deals. Housed in cubicles and representing the diversity of their constituency, they eagerly devoted an average of fourteen hours a day to the campaign.

As she neared the back of the open space, her eyes drifted towards the suite of private offices, her smile deepening when she sensed that Michael was in. Anxious to see him, she made a sharp detour towards his office.

Jennifer stood at his open doorway and peered in on the intense scene. Michael's campaign manager Jerry Weiss was standing behind him looking over his shoulder. His horn-rimmed reading glasses were perched precariously on the bridge of his nose; his prematurely gray hair was raked back off his unshaven face.

Jennifer knocked, alerting the two heads bent in

intense discussion to her presence. "Good morning, Jerry, Michael."

Michael and Jerry looked up at the same time.

"Good morning, Jennifer," Jerry said first.

Michael, looking grim-faced and sounding worn, chimed in. "Yes. Good morning."

"Long night, huh?" Jennifer asked.

"Something like that," Michael stated unconvincingly.

Sensing his vulnerability, Jennifer asked, "Can I help?"

After a brief, tense silence, Jerry voiced Michael's thoughts. "Thanks Jennifer, I'm sure Michael will fill you in later."

Michael managed a nod, his stare intense. "Yes, I'll stop by your office this afternoon, Jennifer. Okay?"

"Sure, Michael," she said, confused by the quick dismissal. Shaking her head, Jennifer walked briskly on to her office, alarmed by the scene she'd just witnessed. Michael hadn't even tried to mask his apprehension, which was unsettling, given his usual fearlessness.

Jennifer turned on her computer and retrieved the fifty e-mails that waited for her. A series of reminders popped up on her screen. As she clicked off the notices, she remembered that Maxine, Michael's press secretary, was coming in at ten. Maxine made it her business to know everything that happened in connection with the campaign and she was quick to spread rumor when she didn't have all the facts. No, Maxine would be thrilled to share whatever she knew, or thought she knew, in tedious detail. She wouldn't even have to ask Maxine. The woman would bop into her office wound tight with news.

Looking at her watch, Jennifer jotted down the things she wanted to accomplish in the hour she had to herself. Answer e-mails. Check on the latest table count for the gala in Hartford. Send out thank you notes to the host and hostesses of the last cocktail parties. She got to work and by nine, she was on top of the busy day that lay in front of her and was reviewing the seating chart for the upcoming gala when Maxine walked in with her hands perched on her hips and talking fast.

"Hey girl. I just got off the phone with a reporter from the *Hartford Courant*. He was mighty audacious. Acted like he's got some secret goods on Michael. He had the nerve to want to feel me out without giving me a clue as to what was going on. Then I stopped by Michael's office and he and Jerry were all huddled up and not sharing either. What's going on? Is this a just-for-males-only party or am I the only one left out?"

Jennifer laughed out loud. She was as curious as Maxine but not up for a gossip session. "Sit down, Maxine. I don't have a clue what's germinating in Michael's office, but I'm sure we'll know soon." She pointed to the armchair opposite her desk. "I'm focused on this dinner, which, may I remind you, is in forty-eight hours. We've got some problems with the seating."

Maxine slumped into the chair. "Well, I'm pissed. I don't know about you, but how am I supposed to do my job when they're holding stuff back from me?" She cursed under her breath.

"Get a grip, Maxine, and take a look at this seating chart. We've got the governor sitting next to the mayor and you know how they despise each other. We've got to break them up. Give each of them their own table. Which means some serious shuffling of the $50,000 tables. Got any ideas?"

Jennifer thrust the papers in front of Maxine, thankful to get her off the topic of Michael, despite her own curiosity. There was something about the woman that she didn't trust. Perhaps it was that Maxine was completely self-serving. Still, Maxine, at forty-five, had been in the world of politics longer than anyone else on the team. Her opinion was usually considered invaluable in some areas. So why wouldn't they want her input now? Damn! She didn't need this intrigue right now with the biggest fundraiser to date on the line.

"I've got it," Maxine chirped. "Let's move Governor Samuels to table three just to Michael's left and then put Mayor Paxton to his right. Here." She thrust the table diagram in front of Jennifer. "Look. It will give the tables an interesting mix without inciting a riot."

Jennifer agreed. Then together they reviewed the remainder of the seating chart, making the necessary changes. Every table was sold but there was still room to squeeze in another table or two. They anticipated a completely sold-out affair by the end of the day.

With table seating complete, Jennifer and Maxine called the consultants in Hartford and directed their attention to the program. Then Maxine rushed out, but not before she issued a final warning that men were not to be trusted.

Jennifer waved Maxine off with a laugh and set about restoring order from the chaos that had just floated out of her office. Although she didn't trust nor necessarily like the woman, she had come to respect her ability in most things. Deciding to take a moment for herself, Jennifer picked up the phone and dialed the Petersons. Brenda had come home the day before and they'd hung out a little while but hadn't had a chance to talk. Really talk.

"Hey," she said as soon as she heard her best friend's raspy voice.

"Jen?"

"Sorry, did I wake you?"

"What time is it?" She sounded foggy.

"Noon. Call me when you wake up."

Releasing a loud groan, Brenda said, "It's okay. I'm just getting over this jet lag. Last night was fun!"

"It was. It's been too long since we spent any time together."

"Don't remind me. So what's on your agenda for today?"

"I'm finishing up last minute details on this Hartford event. But something's up around here."

"Up? Like what?"

"I'm not sure. Michael promised to come by my office later." Jennifer paused, thinking about Maxine's comments. "He's clearly got something on his mind."

"Besides the fact that he's fallen in love with you?"

"Brenda, don't be ridiculous! Michael's got more important things on his mind than falling in love with anybody right now."

"Okay girlfriend, but I suspect your interest in each other goes beyond him winning an election."

"Brenda, would you please try to stop matchmaking. You've been doing it since high school."

"Yeah, and someday I'm gonna succeed. From what little I know about Mr. Wingate, I'm convinced that he's the one."

"That's great…now, can we move on. Besides, you still haven't told me about Sir Galahad."

Brenda laughed. "His name is Tom King. There's not much to tell unless I decide to move to London. He's certainly not moving to the States."

"And why not?"

" 'Cause he's got commitments. You know—kids, an ex-wife, book tour."

"How old is he, Bren?"

"Thirty-seven."

"And how old are his kids?"

"Tom, Jr. is five. His daughter Kim is three. They're great kids," Brenda added as if she needed to convince her friend that it was okay for her to be dating a divorced man with two children.

"So you get along with them okay?"

"Yes, just fine actually. Tom has his children every other weekend."

"Then you are serious about this relationship. I mean, if you're involved with the kids and all, you've got to be thinking long-term."

"I guess. That's what I've got to figure out while I'm home, Jen. Living in London is a whole different world. I have no family or history there. My life is here. Well, part of it anyway. I do miss Tom terribly."

"Bren, why don't you drive up to Hartford with me tomorrow? I could use the company and the help at the affair. It would give us time to talk, plus you'd get a chance to see Michael in action. What do you say?"

"Jen," Brenda whined, "I just got home..."

"I know but it's only for two days. We'll drive up in the morning...the event's Wednesday night and we'll return Thursday morning."

After a brief moment of silence, Brenda softened. "All right. That may be the only way I get to spend time with you anyway."

"Thanks. I'll pick you up about eight. Get some rest and tell your mom that we're going to figure out our love lives and she'll send you off without a fuss!" They laughed together.

Catching her breath, Brenda added, "Mom's a hoot isn't she?"

"You got that right. But I love her dearly."

"Me, too. Speaking of moms, how are things between you, Sarah and Moses?"

"Touchy, but Dad's hired a private investigator. We should be getting some information soon and everyone's nervous. But at least we're all talking about our feelings and I'm proud of how far we've come as a family. Mom's been using this time to teach me about patience. She thinks we will all need it once we find my sister. I guess she's most worried about how the girl will react and she doesn't want us to just show up on her doorstep—thirty years too late."

"She's got a point, you know."

"I guess." She paused to mull over the idea.

"It must be pretty tense around your house."

"We're all so busy that there's not much time for tension, just quick updates. Besides, Dad's so excited that I'm all into this campaign that he's practically dancing around the house. I consult with him on everything, so it's kind of like we're working together. You know, Bren, I think he's proud of me."

"He's always been proud of you, Jennifer. Even when we were kids performing a rock concert on the lawn. Do you remember the summer Irene Cara came out with Fame and we pretended to be famous singers and dancers?"

Laughing at the memory, Jennifer added, "And you wore your mother's stilettos and they kept getting stuck in the grass!"

"What about you in that micro mini…your long

shapely legs twisting to the beat…girl, we had some good days." Brenda let out a hoot that stung Jennifer's ears and sent her into near hysterics.

As the laughter subsided, Jennifer got serious. "Look, I've got to get off this phone. I love you, Brenda."

"I love you too, Jen."

"See you in the morning."

"It'll be fun—that's if I can just get my dead ass in gear."

"Yes, you lazy thing. See you soon."

Getting on with her day, Jennifer spent an hour returning calls and working on the gala. It was nearly dark outside before she took a break. Things were moving in her direction. They were working together as a family to find her sister, Michael's chances of winning the election were looking good, she'd met her campaign goal, and, like it or not, she might be falling in love.

She suddenly felt nauseous. She had planned on going back to L.A. after the three months but now she hated the thought of leaving Michael. Was she ready to give up the West Coast and stay around to give them more time together? Did he feel as strongly as she did? If Michael won, he'd be moving to D.C. Was she willing to be the wife of a U.S. Senator and have to share her husband with a demanding public? What about her work? Her privacy? Cradling her head in her hands, Jennifer closed her eyes and tried to calm her brain with meditation.

Across the suite, Michael paced. He had no idea how to tell Jennifer. The thought of losing her respect made him cringe. Still, he knew that the news had to come from him. He couldn't risk her reading the morning edition of the *Hartford Courant*.

Michael shoved his hands into the deep pockets of his Karl Everett trousers. He'd told Moses the night before that the newspapers were planning to print a lead story claiming that he'd had a baby out of wedlock. Moses had been very angry that he hadn't told him about Max as soon as he'd heard from Daphne three weeks earlier. Michael had no real defense yet he'd argued for his right to process the news in private.

Once the explosion calmed, Moses stressed to Michael that he'd chosen public life and therefore had to accept the responsibility that accompanied it. Michael had listened and reaffirmed his commitment to serve. At that point, the two men had shaken hands and agreed to continue working together. Jerry arrived when they were in the midst of strategizing. The three them had stayed up all night mapping out an elaborate contingency plan. They'd also agreed on a media and advertising appeal that was to be implemented over a five-week period.

Early that morning, Michael had gone to the gym, showered and headed to his office. He was taking a day off from politicking to deal with his situation. Situation…Michael cursed aloud. It was time to stop thinking of his son as a situation. His son, he thought, shaking his head. Michael kicked the corner of the black leather couch angrily as he passed.

He wasn't sure who he was most angry with, himself or Daphne. He should have gone to see her the moment she called instead of letting three weeks pass. But it had been such a shock.

At first, Michael had found it difficult to refocus on his campaign, but within forty-eight hours, he had pushed the question of his paternity onto the back burner until a week later when he received the letter from her attorney threatening a lawsuit for child support.

Backed against the wall, Michael had fired off the first check and called his own lawyer. Then two days ago the call had come in from a reporter. Assuming that Daphne had called the press, he'd pleaded for a forty-eight hour reprieve while they waited for the results of his DNA testing. He had twenty-four hours left.

Angry as he was, Michael was lucid enough to question her motivation in alerting the press. Daphne was a successful photojournalist and a friend since college. He just didn't see why she'd want to destroy either of their careers or inflict such public pain on their families. But in twenty-four hours it wouldn't matter who'd informed the press, he mused. The one-sided story was about to wreak havoc on his campaign and, more importantly, his life.

Michael peered out of his open door towards Jennifer's office. He felt an uncharacteristic tightening in his chest.

Jennifer's reaction to the news meant a great deal to him. He wasn't sure when it had happened but he was pretty certain that he was in love with her. Which made the hypocrisy of his actions all the more pitiful. He'd avoided telling her about his son by convincing himself that he was waiting for the right moment. Truth was, there had been several. He'd just been afraid of losing her. He couldn't believe the irony between his situation now and the decision Moses had made thirty years ago. Jennifer was bound to feel betrayed. Now he'd have to face her wrath and hope that with time he'd regain her respect and trust. Until then he'd have to deal with her hurt feelings and pray that she wouldn't quit the campaign and head west.

Michael stood back, cowardly watching her office from a distance. Somehow, he vowed, he'd make her understand. As he contemplated his next move, he thought back to the talk he'd had with his mother. It had gone well enough. She'd been shocked, of course, but ultimately supportive and full of suggestions on how he should handle the news. But his mother knew him better than Jennifer and didn't need to be convinced that he was still a man of character. As similar thoughts continued to flow through Michael's mind, he moved in the direction of Jennifer's office, hating the pain he was about to inflict. Without a definite plan in mind, he entered her office unannounced.

Jennifer welcomed his interruption. Smiling warmly, she offered him a seat. "Come in, I was just going over the figures for the gala and could use a break from the numbers. Looks good though. We should net over a million," she reported proudly, pushing away from her desk.

He closed the door behind him. "You're incredible. I mean, the way you waltzed in here seven weeks ago and quickly made yourself an invaluable member of the team." Sensing trouble, Jennifer eased out of her desk chair. "Save the flattery until after the gala. If it's half the success we anticipate, there'll be plenty to celebrate." Gesturing towards a pair of armchairs, Jennifer dropped into one, watching Michael closely as he eased into the other. "What's up, Michael?"

Sitting on the edge of the chair, Michael cleared his throat. He leaned towards her and spoke softly. "Has Moses had any success?"

"Success?" she asked, confused.

"Yes, in locating your sister? You haven't talked about the search lately."

"Oh, that…no. Seems her mother married and left the area without a trace, but let's stay on the subject at hand. Why do you look so distressed?"

Shaking his head, Michael breathed deeply, searching for the best way to describe his situation. Mouth dry, he swallowed. "We need to talk."

"I figured that when you barely looked at me this morning. You usually study me with this intensity that makes me squirm," she said, then regretted her attempt to lighten the moment. "It's more than that really. Call it intuition, but Maxine picked up on it also. There's something going on that you're keeping from me…us," she corrected. "So, talk to me."

Michael shifted uncomfortably, toying with his fingers.

In his eyes, Jennifer read something very troubling. Fear. Softening her voice, she tried again. "This isn't like you, Michael. You're usually so cool. So, I'll ask again. What's up?"

Michael couldn't stand her scrutiny. He turned away from the trust in her puzzled eyes. It had taken weeks for her to get to that level and he was about to blow it all in a few minutes. Too nervous to remain still, he rose fluidly and walked away from her.

She watched, concern mounting. Feeling at a loss for words or actions that would ease the burden his shoulders carried, she fought an impulse to go to him and take him into her arms. Instead, she shifted back into her seat and waited.

Michael was silent for a while, struggling for courage. He circled the office for a second time. "I need to talk with you, but I don't know where to begin." He sounded apologetic.

"Just say it, Michael."

Michael swept the room once more before taking a seat. Anxiously, he toyed with his father's gold insignia ring that his mother had given to him on the day his father died.

He raised his eyes to meet her concerned gaze. "The press is threatening to come out with a story that could hurt my campaign."

Frowning, she pressed. "About?"

"About me...my private life... Jennifer, some things may come out..." Michael hesitated.

"Go on," she said softly, adding, "Whatever it is, Michael, I'd rather hear it from you."

"I understand...and I want that too. It's just..." Michael shook his head regretfully. "Jennifer, I...I haven't told you..." His voice sounded tired, strained.

Suspicious, Jennifer stood up and moved away with growing impatience.

"I'll be meeting later with Jerry and Maxine. We need to talk before tomorrow morning."

"Okay, Michael, enough drama. What's going on. We're together, let's talk now," she insisted, her hands perched belligerently on her hips.

"A story is going to break tomorrow morning and we're trying to squelch it. Can't go into details now."

"What's the story?" Jennifer relaxed a bit, thinking the problem political.

"Not now, Jenny." Her office wasn't the place to tell her that he'd fathered a baby and was about to be labeled a deadbeat dad. "And not here. Where will you be later?"

"Later?"

"Say around nine."

"I should be at home. Why?"

"I'll stop by."

"Michael, what's going on?"

"Now isn't the time for us to go into it. I'll call you before I come over, okay?"

Jennifer walked behind her desk. She felt personally threatened but had nothing to base that feeling on. Why was Michael having such a hard time getting the words out? Was it something that affected her directly? She swiveled and faced the window as she struggled to hide her concern. Needing to do something to bridge the gap that had just formed between them, Michael took swift strides towards her and with one strong grasp, he spun her around and pulled her roughly to him. The intent look in his eyes frightened her more than her own thoughts.

Surprised, Jennifer took a deep, unsteady breath. "Michael...," she began.

"Yes, Jenny."

His nearness was making her crazy. "I'm worried," she said softly, her heart pounding erratically.

His long hands took Jennifer's face and stroked her cheeks, sending warm shivers through her. "Me too." Before she had time to protest, he leaned down and brushed his lips over hers, deepening the kiss as she struggled against him.

She felt her knees weaken as Michael's tongue traced her soft full lips, then plunged deeper, exploring, tasting, arousing desire. Her heart pounded wildly as she struggled to gain control. "Michael...stop." She pushed Michael away just as someone knocked on the door.

Michael opened the door and found his assistant on the other side.

"Michael, excuse me…," Betty said apologetically.

"It's okay, Betty. What's up?"

"Attorney Williams is on the phone. He says it's urgent."

"Thanks, Betty. Talk with you later, Jennifer," Michael flung over his shoulder as he walked out.

Still reeling from the kiss, Jennifer stood behind her desk staring straight ahead. Just like that, she mused. Michael had walked in, said nothing really, kissed her dizzy, then run off. "I'll see you later, all right," she repeated to herself in annoyance. "Damn him! Who does he think he is! Maxine was correct. The boys were off dealing with the real crisis and leaving the women to plan the parties and bring in the dollars. Well, she wasn't having any of it. She began to pace restlessly, imagining all kinds of scenarios that might account for Michael's secretive behavior. Men! She was tempted to call her father but figured he'd tell her not to worry because the men were on it! Whatever it was! Her eyes quickly read through her new e-mails. There were five messages about the Hartford gala, all reassuring. Clicking on MichaelWingate.com, she checked the latest poll results that still gave Michael a substantial lead. Maybe there was something else going on that hadn't tested public opinion yet. Election day was less than five weeks away. Public opinion was often fickle as the campaign reached its final moments. Still searching, she scanned the political news flashes that gave up-to-the minute reports and found nothing alarming there. She hopped into a political chat room seeking gossip but clicked it off almost immediately. She was going too far. She had to wait only a few more hours. Patience, that's what her mother would advise her. Be patient, Jennifer, the storm will pass. But which storm, she wondered as her heart pressed against her ribs, making it difficult to breathe.

She was convinced that Michael was hiding something from her that was going to affect her personally. He'd practically admitted it. "I haven't told you everything…"

Jennifer put a Whitney Houston CD into the computer and stewed over her predicament as she listened. She was in love. She almost laughed. The signs had all been there. The joy she felt at the sound of his voice or seeing his name pop up on her caller ID. The rush she felt when they shared the same space. The physical ache she felt deep in her when he'd been gone too long. Touching her hand to her chest, she took a deep breath, trying to slow the thundering inside.

What could have happened that would have Michael so worried, she asked herself again. As a million scenarios jumped into her head, she pitted each against her love for Michael, wondering which one would be most damaging and how much of herself she was willing to sacrifice.

Whitney sang "Same Script, Different Cast" softly in the background. Hearing one of her favorite tunes,

Jennifer reached over and turned the volume up a notch. Was Michael about to tell her about another woman? She caught her breath as her heart skipped a beat. It was always about another woman. But he'd said it could hurt his campaign. Maybe, she reconsidered, that wasn't what he had to tell her. Her mind went into overdrive. Something about his finances maybe. Or his family. She forced herself to stop imagining the worst. Michael had promised to talk with her before the story hit. She would just have to wait until that evening.

Jennifer sang along with Whitney. Her fingertips touched her lips. She smiled, remembering his kiss as Whitney asked if she could have her lover's kiss forever...

Six

T wenty-four hours, he repeated to himself, before he had to justify his failure to control one of the most important aspects of his life. He had a son by a woman he wasn't in love with but might be expected to marry. "Damn!" Michael uttered repeatedly, slamming his right fist into the palm of his left hand.

He couldn't believe the trick fate had played on him. Just when he was nearing his goals, he was at great risk of blowing it all. He thought over his all-nighter with Moses and Jerry. They'd helped him map out his political response but only he could determine his moral obligation. Michael considered his options. Drop out of the campaign citing personal reasons? Marry the mother of his firstborn because it was the honorable thing to do? Not to mention the fact that marriage would be the easiest way to save his political career. Face the cameras confident, compassionate, responsible and refuse to address publicly his personal affairs...refuse to back down.

He cursed, kicking the leg of his desk until his toe screamed back at him in stabs of pulsating pain. Why did Daphne wait to tell him about the baby until he could almost smell victory? he asked selfishly.

He'd gone over their years of friendship many times in his head. Daphne was an independent, strong-willed and ambitious woman but not mean-spirited or manipulative. Yet her timing couldn't have been worse for his political career. So again he asked himself, why now? And what did she expect from him? Marriage?

The DNA test results were due back that afternoon, but that had only been a stall tactic buying him a day or two before public disgrace. He knew what he had to do before his time was up.

His political opponents were going to have a field day when they found out. They'd claim that Michael preached one set of standards for others and held himself to less stringent ones. He imagined the deep plunge the polls would take by the time the news of his out-of-wedlock paternity hit the papers.

Michael swore under his breath. He was determined that his private life would not be the reason he lost the election.

Max, he mused. He liked the name and was getting used to the idea that he had a son whom he'd yet to lay eyes on.

Knowing what he had to do, Michael grabbed his phone off the cradle and dialed Jerry's extension. "I need to see you and Maxine, now. We'll meet in my office," he shouted into the phone.

Within ten minutes, he'd briefed his key staffers and had begun packing his briefcase. "Send a memo telling the staff that no one is to speak to the press. All calls should be forwarded to either you or Maxine," Michael said.

Jerry nodded. "Shall we prepare a release? It's the only way we can control the content."

"I don't know. Maxine, what do you think?"

"Michael, I agree with Jerry. This is going to be tricky. We need to be prepared, especially with the Hartford fundraiser coming up. Which reminds me. Have you spoken to Jennifer?"

He shook his head. "I've spoken to her. I just haven't told her about the baby yet." He paused. "I'm going to go over to her house later so we can talk." Turning back to Jerry, Michael asked, "Gut feeling, Jerry, can we survive this scandal?"

"Depends on you, Michael. You'll be watched, closely, to see how you respond to this crisis. So before the story breaks, I suggest you take a few hours to think this through."

"Actually, I'm going to see the baby," Michael stated

emphatically.

Maxine jumped up. "What? When?"

"Right now," Michael replied.

"But what about the DNA test results? Shouldn't you wait until we get them back?"

He looked at Maxine and said, "I doubt if Daphne would lie about this. The boy is most likely mine, Maxine. I think I'll know when I see him. If he is, I've waited long enough. I'm not going to wait any longer." Moving on, he barked orders. "Jerry, get someone to rush the test results or either way we'll be reacting to a story without the full facts."

"Our sources tell us that we'll have the results within an hour," Jerry answered.

"Good. Call me on my cell phone. What's our deadline with the *Hartford Courant*."

"I spoke with the chief editor, Mark Sanford. They're giving us until ten. If they don't hear from us by then, they'll run the story as is. Unless you want to grant them an interview."

"No interview. Look, this is my personal business and I have no intention of spinning some soap opera that will haunt me and my son for life. Maxine, get the release ready, two versions...you understand. Can you two hold down the office for a few hours? I'll be back by six."

"Of course," Jerry and Maxine replied.

"Michael, I'm so sorry this happened this way...," Maxine said.

He smiled, appreciative of their loyalty. "Thank you…for your support, loyalty and advice." He stood and prepared to leave. "I've got to get out of here. Jerry, Maxine, thank you, again," he called over his shoulder, already halfway out of the door.

Maxine waved. "Good luck."

Jerry stood. "Now get out of here! We'll meet with the staff."

Michael smiled. "You know how to reach me."

As Michael pulled his car onto the highway, he called Daphne.

"Daphne."

"Yes."

"It's Michael."

"I know."

"I'm on my way to your house. I want to see my son."

Following seconds of silence, he asked, "Daphne? Is this a bad time for me to be stopping by?"

In a voice that sounded shaky, she responded, "No, Michael. We'll be here." She then gave him directions.

"See you in twenty." Michael hung up and breathed deeply. He felt oddly at peace, ready to face the truth. Trying to maintain his composure, Michael focused his attention on getting through the heavy traffic on Interstate 95. He was headed north to Fairfield. Maneuvering into the fast lane, his thoughts drifted back to the baby. He tried to imagine what Max would look like.

His heart raced as he exited the highway and began

weaving his way along unfamiliar roads. He'd just turned onto Applebee Lane, where Daphne and Max lived, when his cell phone rang.

He listened in silence as the director explained that they rarely agreed to give results over the telephone. Michael thanked the voice on the phone for his under-standing and willingness to break with policy this once. Then he listened calmly as the director told him what he was already prepared to accept. Max was indeed his son. He thanked the man again and turned in at 121 Applebee. Michael sat in the car a minute gathering his composure. He let out a deep sigh as the weight of his new responsibil-ity hit him hard.

Michael peered around Daphne looking for signs of his son. "Where's Max," he asked gruffly.

"Taking a nap." She stepped aside so that Michael could enter the house, then closed the door and suggested that they go into the living room. While Daphne filled the strained silence with a litany of missed moments in their son's life, Michael picked up Max's scrapbook.

He stiffened when he saw the first picture. Max had chestnut-colored eyes, a square jaw, long limbs and Michael's smile. "He looks a lot like me when I was a baby," he finally voiced.

"Does he?" Watching Michael looking at photos that

chronicled his son's first four months made Daphne feel guilty for denying him the pleasure of those early months. How could her thinking have been so flawed? From this moment on, she vowed in silence, she'd no longer think of Max as just her baby. Her fears that Michael would reject their baby had been so completely unfounded. He was a good man and he'd never given her any reason to believe otherwise.

But there would be changes in their lives. Until this moment, she and Max had been the pair. Now there was a third person to consider. She would have to give up total control, but Max would have both of his parents in his life. Well, maybe. Michael hadn't said that he wanted to be involved. And if he did, certainly their arrangement was destined to be non-traditional. But deep inside she wondered if there was any hope for them to be a family? No, that was unlikely. She'd seen to that when she excluded him from Max's life early on.

Michael stood and walked across the room, struggling with the weight of it all. Wheeling around, he asked, "Why, Daphne?"

Daphne lifted her chin and boldly met Michael's eyes. "Why what, Michael?"

Michael struggled to contain the anger. "Why didn't you tell me as soon as you found out that you were pregnant? Why wait until Max is three months old and my campaign's in full swing?"

Daphne girded herself for his criticism. "It's a long

story."

Michael shot her a penetrating stare. "I've got plenty of time, so let's hear it."

"Damn it, Michael! We've been friends since college."

He frowned with cold fury. "So you decided that it was okay to have my baby?"

"No!" she shouted, angrily jerking to her feet and moving stiffly to the opposite side of the room, presenting her back to him. Staring out into the backyard, comforted by the familiar surroundings, she pulled in her emotions. He was right. She owed him an explanation. Determined, she swiveled to face her baby's father squarely. "I didn't exactly plan to get pregnant, Michael...just didn't take any precautions against it."

"But you told me you had," Michael countered.

Daphne looked at him directly. "I'd been on Depo Provera for years and my cycle was all screwed up."

"Depo Provera? What is that? I thought you were taking the pill?"

"No, I never said what kind of birth control I was using. Depo Provera is a hormone injection that I get every three months. I was in between shots and I hadn't had a period in six months. Since I wasn't sexually active, well, until that night with you, I hadn't been worried about getting pregnant. Anyway, I finally went to the doctor and discovered that I was pregnant." Calmer now, she took slow deliberate steps towards Michael. "I was in Somalia. It was a terrible time...but I finished the assignment and flew back to New York." Daphne paused. "I thought about calling you, Michael, but you'd just announced your candidacy, and the last thing either of us needed was some kind of scandal. Besides, I hadn't seen or spoken to you in months. So, I wasn't willing to take the risk of calling you up one Sunday morning and saying, "Oh, by the way, our little reunion resulted in a pregnancy. Besides, I hadn't even accepted the fact that I was having a baby yet…I couldn't imagine you wanting anything to do with it either."

Eyes filled with contempt, Michael glared at Daphne. "So you just waited until Max was three months old to tell me instead? Give me a break, Daphne."

She shot back a wicked look. "And you waited nearly a month to come and see your child!"

"Need I remind you that you had nine months to adjust to motherhood?" he retorted, refusing to let her know how guilty he'd been feeling.

"What do you want from me, Michael? It was an error in judgement, okay? The whole thing. I should have called you after I decided to go through with the pregnancy, but I wonder if your reaction would have been any different. Would you have been willing to accept the pregnancy and be there with me when Max was born? I doubt it."

"I don't know," he replied honestly. "I can't say what I would have done. I can only deal with today."

"And I couldn't have dealt with my pregnancy and my disappointment in you at the same time. I refused to go through the humiliation that my mother went through when she told my biological father about her pregnancy with me. I thought of everything, including the fact that I never met my biological father. So, I did it my way. Alone."

Tension swirled around them as they studied each other in silence.

"Daphne, you ought to know me well enough to know that I'd want to share in that decision right from the beginning..."

"I had no idea how you'd react to my pregnancy. Besides it wasn't your body involved, nor your career. So I made the decision on my own."

Michael started to interrupt her, but she held up her hands motioning to him to stop. "It wasn't easy, Michael." Daphne paused, staring blankly past Michael. "As I was developing the photos from Somalia, seeing again the effects of drought, war and famine, the faces of malnourished women and children, disease, make-shift camps and orphaned babies, I acknowledged my blessings...the pregnancy was one of them. I decided at that moment to maintain the pregnancy and raise the baby, even if it meant doing it on my own. The next day I registered for prenatal care and heard the baby's heartbeat for the first time. By then you were heavy into campaign mode." Eyes weary, Daphne met Michael's cool gaze steadily. "Damn it, Michael, you were all caught up in this run for the senate. If I'd bounced into your life fat with a child you would have freaked out and, God knows, said what? I...I couldn't take that risk."

"What risk, Daphne?"

"The risk that you'd reject me at a point when I was totally vulnerable. As the pregnancy progressed, I got stronger. Felt more and more capable of raising the baby on my own. I'd made enough money to support myself for a year. Who knows, maybe a part of me was trying to prove something. After all, my mother managed alone until she met my stepfather. She learned the hard way about the price you pay when you have no resources and your dignity is compromised. I wasn't going to let that happen to me."

"Just like that. You thought it was okay to make all the decisions. Not give me any say. Damn, Daphne! How selfish!"

Hands on hips, Daphne refused to back down even though she was beginning to feel uneasy under his scrutiny. "Can I go on? Please?"

Michael nodded slowly.

"I was plenty scared at first. I considered calling you again the day Max and I got home. He was the most beautiful creature I'd ever seen and yet I felt sad because there was no father there to share the moment with. What I hadn't counted on was the strain the decision would have on me emotionally. I cried for the next ten days, too proud to tell anyone how scared I really was. Mom found me one afternoon during a crying jag and insisted that I come home with her that afternoon. Max and I stayed with my parents until he was six-weeks-old. Then we moved back here.

"From the start, I didn't even want anyone to know that you were the baby's father. At first, my parents pressed me to reveal the name of the man who'd left me pregnant. My mother said that I wasn't being fair to Max or to myself. But I wouldn't back down. I didn't want them interfering or going to you." She looked up into his cold eyes and tried again to make him understand. "I knew that it wasn't love between us, Michael, and I didn't want a sense of duty or political pressure to kick in and force us to do something that wouldn't work—for either of us. I figured that I could keep the baby a secret until after the elections. I knew that it was a risk but I was determined to stick by my plan." *Michael* stared at Daphne, trying to absorb without anger what she was trying to tell him. "Your little plan didn't work, did it?"

"No."

Michael grabbed Daphne's arm. "Daphne, we've been friends for too long. Hard as you've tried to play it off as insignificant, I've seen signs of how much it bothers you not to know who your biological father was and not to really understand why he was never a part of your life. Of course, your mother married when you were a little girl and your stepfather's been great, but it doesn't make up for the loss you've been feeling all these years. Am I right?"

She started to object but couldn't. He was right. "Yes and no. I don't think I missed not having a father in my life during those early years."

"The early years are the most formative in a child's life, Daphne. You know that. But that's beside the point. I guess we both used poor judgement," he conceded. Toying with the change in his pockets, he paced. Then Michael stopped pacing and turned again to her. "Go on with your story."

"I took Max for his well-baby checkup. I was filled with guilt and tired of all the deception. When Dr. Smith was doing the history, he kept asking all these questions about Max's father. I tried evading them but he talked with me about the importance of knowing the medical history of both parents. I tried telling him all I knew about your background without revealing who you were. Finally I broke down. He was my doctor as well, so I've known him for many years. His kindness got me through some rough moments as a kid so I felt safe opening up to him. I told him that you were Max's father. Dr. Smith listened without voicing a judgement. Then he calmly convinced me that I should talk to my parents and consider notifying you."

"And…?" Michael pressed, not willing to let up until his questions were answered satisfactorily.

"I told my mother and stepfather that night. I explained that you knew nothing about the pregnancy or Max's birth. We argued for days about telling you. I told them that I wanted to wait until after the campaign. Mom said it couldn't wait. She was livid. My stepfather wanted to tell you himself. For a while there he was completely irrational, acting as if you had deserted Max and me. I felt like a child again. The more I tried to regain control, the more they insisted that I contact a lawyer and force you to do the right thing."

"I didn't need your parents to tell me to provide for my child!" Michael protested angrily.

"I know that, Michael, but my parents don't know you like I do. Give them a break. Dad remembered the pain my mother was in when he met her and assumed it was the same with me. When I objected, he fumed. He swore that I was behaving selfishly and being immature to think that I could raise a baby all by myself. Mom retreated into the past. I think the stress brought back all kinds of painful memories of her pregnancy with me. For the first time she told me about her feelings when she was pregnant with me. It was painful hearing her story. She pleaded with me to involve you in Max's life as soon as possible. Mom got to me..." Daphne swept her fingers nervously through the mass of short curly hair. "I called you right after that."

Still skeptical, Michael retorted, "And when I didn't respond immediately you called the papers, right?"

Daphne stared in disbelief. "Now why would I do anything that stupid to our child? Damn you, Michael. I just told you that I didn't even want to tell my parents. I left the hospital with the name of my baby's father left blank on his birth certificate. Do you have any idea how humiliating that was? So why would I put our messy business out there for public consumption? No," she shouted angrily, "I did not call the papers!"

"Then who called them?" Michael asked, perplexed.

"I don't know. I learned about the leak to the press when a reporter from the *Courant* called me and asked if the story was true. I refused to confirm or deny that Max was your son. I was furious, too. I accused my parents of calling the newspaper but they swore they had nothing to do with it. I have no idea who called the press, Michael. Really. Can we squelch the story somehow?"

Michael saw only sincerity in the striking pair of eyes that stared back at him. "I doubt it. We got them to hold off until I got back the DNA test results but that was just a tactic to buy us some time. They'll probably run the story tomorrow morning." Michael slumped onto the sofa, head pressed between his hands. He started talking softly without looking up. "I didn't believe you at first, Daphne, but then I thought about it and I realized that you wouldn't lie to me about something this important. Then I guess anger set in. I felt robbed of something so important to me. Can you understand?"

Michael froze as he heard his son's cry for the first time.

"I better go check on Max," Daphne said without answering his question.

She returned and handed Max to his father without a word.

Michael's lips formed a broad smile as he accepted the chubby four-month-old boy into his arms. His eyes took a moment to scan his son's soft brown eyes, round caramel face, head full of bubbly curls.

Max settled quickly in his father's arms as if he weren't a stranger. His eyes explored Michael's face while his fingertips toyed with his nose, mouth and chin. Michael let the boy play, fighting back the tears that formed in his eyes as he realized that this amazing creature was his son.

Daphne stepped back, observing the father-son bonding. Eyes misty, she whispered, "I'm sorry."

Michael, flooded with emotion, glanced in Daphne's direction. "He's so beautiful, Daphne. Until now, he wasn't real to me. Oh, it's hard to explain..."

Daphne returned his smile. "I understand."

Max began to fret and reach towards his mother.

Daphne smiled at Michael. "He's hungry," she said, taking her baby into her arms and settling back into the sofa. Max nestled into the crock of her arms and rooted for the source of his milk and comfort. She glanced over at Michael, then discreetly lifted her T-shirt and settled Max onto her left breast. While her baby suckled, she played with his soft chubby hands and avoided Michael's gaze.

Michael could see that the baby was content attached to his mother's breast. It was a beautiful sight yet the unfamiliar intimacy made him uncomfortable. He stood and walked over to the piano, pretending to study the framed photographs. Actually, he was deep in thought. He knew that this meeting with Daphne had gone well enough and he felt pretty certain that she'd stay on his side. But what of the campaign? He turned just as Max released his hold on Daphne and looked towards his father. Michael smiled warmly.

"I guess I handled this very badly," Daphne said.

He managed a soft smile. "Maybe we both did. So, what's next?"

"I'm not sure but I know that I want my baby...our baby," she corrected, "to know that both his parents love him deeply even though we've chosen to live separately. What did you have in mind?"

Michael faced her. "I need to give it some thought, given the complexity of our lives, but I think it would be best for Max to be raised by both of us. When do you have to go back to work?"

"In six months."

"That will give me time to get things set up," he said.

"What are you talking about?"

"I think that a joint custody arrangement would be best," he stated emphatically.

Joint custody? She hadn't considered that option. The thought of it threatened her. She struggled to find her voice. "I see. I'm not ready to go there, Michael."

Michael's expression didn't change. "Look, Daphne, let's get this straight," he continued with quiet firmness. "I'll only accept a joint parenting arrangement. That's the bottom line. And I'll fight you until I win."

"If you do win the senate seat, won't you have a residence here and in D.C.?"

"Yes."

"The dual residency is too disruptive for a baby."

"I can hire a nanny," he threw out in anticipation of her objections. "We'll have to be flexible so Max won't feel like he's being bounced between us but I think some sort of joint custody can be arranged. There will be times when I'll be traveling for a few weeks and would love it if Max were with you. And I'm sure there will be times when you'll need the same kind of flexibility, right?"

"Correct," Daphne responded thoughtfully.

"Will you go back to working for *Time Magazine* or what?"

Daphne studied Michael, then replied, "I think so, depending on what can be worked out with my schedule. My priorities have shifted, so I won't be taking long assignments. I've had some preliminary discussions with the editor-in-chief and I think he's amenable."

It felt odd to be setting up a child's life as if it were a business deal, but Michael plugged on, needing them to settle as many details as possible while they had the time together. "I'll contact my lawyer this afternoon and have him draw up a draft agreement. He'll send you a copy to review with your attorney. Okay?"

Daphne nodded in reluctant agreement. "Yes." Frowning, she continued, "Michael how will you handle the press?"

Michael fixed his eyes on Daphne. "I'm not totally sure yet. I'll probably keep it general. Acknowledge that

Max is my son and that we're working out the custody arrangements. Beyond that I intend on keeping as many of the details as possible out of the public eye. I'd appreciate it if you'd do the same." He eyed her cautiously.

"I want this over as quickly as possible. I'll talk with my parents and get them to buy into our plan to keep Max out of the press. They adore him, Michael. I'm certain that they would hate to think that anything they did caused him harm. But, Michael, do you really think that they'll run the story tomorrow without our input?"

"Of course they'll run it. Have you forgotten that I'm a black man running for the U.S. Senate from Connecticut? Tomorrow I'll be headline news across the state."

"What can I do to help?"

"Just keep our son safe and happy. I'll handle my campaign. I won't have much time to spend with him until after the election but somehow I'll see him each week." Michael stood. "I've got to go. I'll make arrangements to pick up Max next weekend. I'll sit down with your parents at that time to discuss the future. We've been friends for many years, Daphne. Good friends—nothing more. Let's keep it like that."

Daphne returned his smile. "I agree." She pulled herself together and stood with the child in her arms.

Michael kissed his son's forehead and repeated his plans to take Max for a few hours over the weekend. The threesome headed to Michael's car together. Michael hesitated

Sharon Robinson

with one foot resting on the step of his car. He took a last
look at his son, then bent to kiss Daphne on her cheek
before driving off, completely unaware that they were being
photographed.

132

Seven

Jennifer woke at six with a foreboding about Michael's strange behavior. He hadn't even stopped by as he'd promised. Annoyed that he'd been so inconsiderate, she hopped out of bed to shower and dress so that she could get on the road. She tried to shrug off the nagging concern. It had probably been another late night. He was due to arrive in Hartford by three. She'd talk with him then.

At five minutes after seven Jennifer pulled her Sebring into the parking lot of a small shopping center. After retrieving her clothes from the cleaners, she stopped by the deli to get a cup of coffee, bagel and the Connecticut papers. Standing over the newspaper rack, she gasped aloud. Plastered across the front cover of the *Hartford*

Courant was the bold headline, "Senatorial Candidate Michael Wingate Sued for Paternity."

Hands trembling, she picked up the paper and stared at a photo of Michael with a woman who they claimed was the mother of his four-month-old son. Daphne Wade, she repeated aloud, trying to place the name. It didn't even sound familiar. Maybe the story was completely false. That thought stayed with her only briefly as she reminded herself that the *Hartford Courant* was a reputable paper. They wouldn't have printed an article that had no legs.

Baby? Michael's a father? Jennifer stumbled as she took a step backwards. Her eyes scanned the front pages of the other Connecticut papers, looking for confirmation. Finding none, she folded the *Courant*, paid for it, then rushed back to her car to read the article in private. A wave of nausea passed through her as she realized that Michael had lied to her parents, the voters and to her. He'd proven himself to be just like all the other politicians after all. Disappointment turned to anger. Blinded by rage, she fought tears and barely heard her cell phone ring.

✾✦✾

"Jennifer," Michael began. "I'm sorry that I didn't make it over last night. I needed to spend time with my mother and sister. By the time we got through with our family meeting it was after midnight."

"It's true then?" she asked, praying that he would say

the story was untrue,

"I guess you read the paper," he said, recognizing the anger in her voice.

"Yes. Is it true?"

"Mostly."

"You should have told me about the baby when I asked you if you had any skeletons," she said, almost breathless with anger.

"I didn't know then, Jennifer."

"Yeah, right. Do you expect me to believe that?"

"Jennifer, stop. I know this is a shock and a huge disappointment but let me explain."

Jennifer cut in curtly, "So, it's true then. You do have a four-month-old son?"

"Yes, but, Jennifer, it's not like they describe."

Angry, Jennifer attacked instead of listening. "Tell me something, Mr. Wingate. By what moral authority do you speak to others about responsibility when you have obviously failed miserably? Who are you anyway?"

Michael sighed heavily, anguished at the way Jennifer had learned of his paternity. "I understand your anger, Jennifer. I should have told you myself. I intended to when I came into your office yesterday, but I wanted to tell you in private. I'm sorry, but if you'll give me a chance I'll explain…"

Jennifer flung up an arm, then slammed it on the steering wheel. "Explain? To me? The voters? Your mother? My father? Oh God, now that you've been caught in a lie, you want to explain to me?"

"Yes, to you."

"And why is that?"

"Because…," Michael began, then paused, thinking his case futile. "It's important to me that you understand…that's all."

"Look Michael, this is your problem. I'm just your fundraiser…for the next forty-eight hours anyway."

"What do you mean?"

"I mean that my commitment to this campaign ends after I've closed the books on the event in Hartford. That should take me about forty-eight hours. And don't you forget it!" Jennifer felt like hanging up on him but remembered that their primary relationship was business.

"Jennifer, where are you?"

She didn't respond immediately. Couldn't because she was fighting to regain her control. How could she have been so stupid! She'd allowed herself to be drawn in by Michael's charm. Then she'd fallen in love with a man she obviously didn't even know. Her heart ached. Her breathing was ragged. Forcing back the emotion, she prayed for the strength to make it through the next forty-eight hours when she'd have to pretend that she wasn't completely devastated by the news. "I'm in the car ready to drive up to Hartford. We have a major fundraiser tomorrow night, remember?" She bit her lip until it throbbed like her racing pulse.

"Meet me somewhere so we can talk this out."

"Not a chance. I've got to stay focused on this fundraiser. I'll see you in Hartford. Goodbye, Michael." Jennifer flicked her cell phone off, tossing it angrily on the passenger seat. Struggling with her keys, she fought the sensations of sickness and desolation that swept over her. Her breath was shallow, her senses drugged.

Then Jennifer yielded to compulsive sobs that shook her as she admitted to herself that she should never have trusted Michael. As the sobs subsided, she tried to get up the motivation to drive to Hartford when all she really wanted to do was go home, pack her clothes and take the next flight back to Los Angeles. As thoughts of escape raced through her mind, her phone rang.

"Jennifer! We've been trying to reach you. Have you seen the *Hartford Courant* yet?" Maxine spoke rapidly.

"It's sitting next to me. I was hoping you'd say it isn't true."

"Sorry, honey, seems so. DNA results came back yesterday. Our candidate is a dad. A bit of a complication but not insurmountable. Where are you, by the way? He's been trying to reach you."

"I just spoke with him."

"Where are you?"

"I'm in my car about to head to Hartford. Do we go through with the gala?"

"You bet! But Michael's asked us not to talk with the media. He's issuing a release and heading up to Hartford this afternoon. I'm sure he'll brief us later."

"Where is Michael? I was so shocked and angry, I didn't bother to ask him."

"I'm not sure. He needed some space. Let's not jump to conclusions. We don't know the whole story. Michael opted not to give the *Courant* an interview so they went to press with a brief release from us stating that Michael was indeed the baby's father and that he planned to fulfill his obligations to his son."

"What exactly does that mean?"

"Well, I'm not sure since he didn't go into detail with us either. He was pretty shaken when he came back from seeing the baby."

"Do you know Daphne Wade?"

"Never even heard her name mentioned until yesterday. But Michael keeps his private life pretty close to the chest, so it doesn't surprise me that he has a woman in his life."

"They're a couple then?"

"Jenny, this is pure speculation. I don't know a thing about Michael's love life except that he's not married. Look, he's depending on us."

Maxine surprised Jennifer. She was the last person she'd expect to side with Michael. Jennifer sighed. "Yeah. Easy, huh? Don't you feel angry…betrayed, Maxine?"

"Because?"

"Because Michael didn't tell us himself before this story broke. I mean, shouldn't we have been told long ago?"

"Look, Jenny, I told you men can't be trusted. Supposedly Daphne kept the pregnancy from him but then he took his time going to see the baby. I guess she got angry and called the press."

"I don't blame her."

"Yeah. I guess I'd have gone off on him too. But that's not our problem right now. We've got a campaign to hold together. You up for it?"

"I'll get through the gala. After that, I'm not making any promises."

"Okay."

"What will this do to Michael's candidacy?"

"I think the voters will give him some time to sort things out. Then I believe he'll regain their support."

"It's odd. As angry as I am, I still believe he's the best candidate."

"I hear you. Oops, there's my other phone. Got to go. See you in Hartford. And, Jennifer, stay calm. We'll get through this. I know you've busted your ass and this is a downer but don't let it show, okay?"

"I won't."

"Got to go. You sure you're okay with this?" Maxine's concern registered in her voice.

With what? Jennifer thought. The baby? Michael's lie? "I'll be fine. Got to go. We have our last million dollars to raise. Call me if anything comes up. I'll check back in when I get to the hotel. Oh, one more thing. Have you or Jerry spoken with our event organizers?"

"Jerry talked with Susan early this morning. She's cool. We're to proceed like nothing's different."

Impossible, she wanted to say. "See you later, Maxine." Confused, Jennifer drove out of the parking lot heading to Brenda's house. On the way, she switched on Connecticut talk radio, certain that news of Michael's paternity would be the hot topic for the morning. She listened frozen as the callers loudly voiced opinions ranging from so-what-else-is-new to politicians lie to men lie to full support for his candidacy regardless of whether he married the mother of his baby or not. There were a number of callers who flat out denied that he could win given the news and others who felt it made no difference. The calmest voice of reason for that morning came from an elderly woman who insisted that they give the new parents time to adjust to their responsibility. She implied that from the look of the photo, marriage might be an option.

Jennifer gripped the wheel of the car tightly. Marriage. She hadn't thought about that. Tears filled her eyes as she contemplated losing Michael forever.

Eight

As Jennifer drove north on the twisty and lush Merritt Parkway, she put down the top of her convertible and turned on the heat. The overnight thunderstorms had given way to a beautiful, sunny fall morning. Because of the unusually wet summer, the New England foliage was in its full regalia of colors. Low-lying branches with crimson and moss green oak leaves still glistened with rain.

Brenda peered over at her friend and shook her head. Though Jennifer had barely spoken five words, she'd avoided questioning her about her strange mood. Brenda huddled down in her seat, freezing. Unable to get warm, she reached into her black leather satchel and wrapped her mint green pashmina around her head and neck. Her eyes drifted to the speedometer. Jennifer was driving 70 miles per hour in a 55-mile zone.

Jennifer glanced over at Brenda and had to laugh. "Damn girl, you look like you're cold or something."

Scowling, Brenda replied, "Whatever gives you that impression?"

"I'll pull over at the next rest stop and put up the top."

"Not on my account. I'm loving this top-down-crazy-driving thing…just wondering, though, to whom we owe this madness," Brenda shouted, trying to be heard over the blasting music, whistling wind and Jennifer's anxiety.

Jennifer looked over at Brenda and giggled. She was so glad to have her along for comic relief. With the gloved index finger on her right hand, she turned down the volume.

"Look, girl, I have a better idea. We can keep the top down but why don't you just pull over at that rest stop and let me drive before you kill us both!"

"If you're cold, turn up the heat!"

"Cold! I'm beyond cold…it's sixty degrees and with the wind chill it's got to be closer to fifty and you've got the damn top down. Now I ask, who's crazy?"

"Okay, okay. I'll stop and put up the top!"

"No. No, you won't put that disappointment on me. I know you like this insane ride and having the top down is part of it." Brenda turned up the heat and redirected the fan so that the warm air was blowing directly on her.

Jennifer smiled over at Brenda. "I couldn't have made this trip without you. Did I thank you for coming?"

"That's about all you've said to me in twenty minutes. But that was before we got in this rented gold convertible Chrysler Sebring and embarked on this exciting tour of New England fall foliage. Which I'm having a bit of difficulty seeing since we've been traveling at such a high speed. No, my dear friend, you don't owe me a thank you. I want an explanation. What the hell has gotten you so bent out of shape?"

Jennifer looked over at the one person she trusted implicitly. Easing her foot off the accelerator slightly, she breathed in and released the tension from her shoulders as she exhaled. "Michael."

"I figured as much, but what about him? Did you discover a wife hidden away in Haiti or something?" Brenda shot a look at Jennifer.

"Brenda, stop it! It's…"

"It's what? Another woman?"

"Yes and no. Oh, Brenda, it's complicated. Threatening. It could ruin his run for the Senate."

"What could ruin his career? Jennifer, you're not making any sense. Give it to me straight. You've pulled me into the middle of this, so let's hear it."

Biting her lip, Jennifer kept her eyes focused on the road. "You didn't read the Hartford paper this morning?"

"Need I remind you that I'm not a morning person and you picked me up at seven-fifteen? Why? What did I miss?"

"Michael has a baby."

"What?"

Peering over at Brenda's confused expression, she continued, "You heard me. Michael's a dad."

"You just found out?"

"That's right. Read it in the paper this morning. The *Courant's* on the back seat in my briefcase. Get it and you'll understand."

Without saying a word, Brenda did as she was told, gasping out loud as she read the headlines. "I'll be damned! Who is this woman? Did she just come out of the blue and announce to Michael that she had his baby or what? I mean, you've been spending at least twelve hours a day with the man and he never even mentioned that he had a baby." "From what Maxine says, Michael didn't know until just recently. Isn't this a bitch!"

"Well, her timing is perfect. Guess she's aiming for the role of Mrs. Senator Wingate. Nice move. Michael's just the kind who would fall for it too. You know, feel like he's got to marry the woman and make things right with the universe."

Tears welled in Jennifer's eyes. Everything Brenda was saying made sense.

Brenda stared at Jennifer's sad expression. "Oh, my. I see. Damn, girl, this is a mess. What does Michael say about it? The man has been racking up the women voters with his strong stand on women's issues. He better have a good story."

"That's just it. We still haven't really talked so I only

know what I've read and what little Maxine told me."

"If the paper's got the story right, Michael saw the baby for the first time yesterday. The woman's got to be pissed off, especially given the man's public rhetoric. Jennifer, how well do you really know him?"

"My parents have known him for years. Dad's spent more time with this man recently than he has with me. They trust Michael implicitly. Well, at least they used to. I haven't actually spoken to my father since I heard about the baby. Besides, what could he say? He's just as guilty."

"Yeah—more guilty actually since he was a married man. But it makes me wonder how well you know Michael Wingate."

"We've been together twelve, fourteen hours a day for the past seven weeks. I think I know him pretty well!"

"A whole seven weeks, huh?"

Jennifer knew Brenda had shifted into her protective mode, still, the sarcasm in her voice stung. Trying not to sound too defensive, she replied, "I know it sounds like I'm being impulsive...and maybe I am. I've never felt like this before."

"I'm sorry to come down so hard on you, Jennifer. It's so unlike you. Actually, you're acting more like me and God knows I hate to see you get hurt." Brenda squeezed her friend's right hand as it lay near the gearshift.

"Michael can't be in love with the woman!" Jennifer threw out confidently.

"Now wait a minute, girl! It's time you got real.

Michael very well might be in love or at least in love with the idea of being a U.S. Senator. That might mean playing the game right down to marrying the woman he deflowered, if you get my drift. Either way, the situation is bound to reflect badly on his campaign. He'll have to have a genie to pull this one off. But as much as I don't like the sound of this, I'd hear Michael out before making a final judgement. You owe him that much."

Jennifer gave Brenda's words some thought, then said, "I just don't understand, Brenda. Why didn't Michael come clean on this before the story broke? Why is it just now blowing up? Seems to me like the woman has a full agenda, like trapping Michael into marriage or something." "I agree. There must be something more to the story."

"I'll bet she didn't know who the baby's father was," Jennifer offered.

"Did Michael say anything about getting DNA testing?"

"I didn't let him talk about it, actually, but Maxine said he'd just got the results back yesterday. I assume they were positive or the *Courant* wouldn't have run with the story."

"Jennifer, I wonder if this Daphne woman held off on telling Michael because she didn't want to deal with rejection. You know women do things like that. We're so used to just dealing, being strong, accepting whatever comes our way. Maybe she's just that capable. Says in this article that she's an award-winning photojournalist. Maybe marriage is not on her agenda at all."

"I guess it's possible. Michael asked me to meet him so we could talk, but I blew him off. I needed some time to work out my feelings on this before seeing him. Does that make sense?"

"Totally. But on the other hand, how are we going to know what you'll be facing when we hit Hartford if you don't speak with him?"

"Maxine will alert me if there's danger ahead. If I haven't heard from her before then, I'll call the office once we check into the hotel, before we hook up with the consultants. We're only about twenty minutes outside of the city."

"Jen, what if Michael plans on marrying his baby's mother?"

The thought was sobering. Jennifer shot an anguished look at Brenda. "It would be best for his career, I suppose," she admitted sadly. "Truth is, I don't know how he'll react. I don't even know if his campaign can survive the scandal if he doesn't propose marriage."

"Well, let's take just one of those questions. Would it change the way you feel about Michael if he doesn't propose marriage?"

"Depends."

"On what?"

"How he deals with his baby, I guess."

"Um…good answer."

"Truthfully, it's not the campaign that I'm worried about being in jeopardy. Michael has a distinct lead on his opponent. He's always been straightforward with the people, so I think they'll ultimately support him. He stepped forward and publicly acknowledged his child. After all, it's a child we're talking about here, not some fatal flaw. At least, I don't see it as one. He hasn't really compromised his position on the importance of male accountability."

"That's good. So what are you worried about?"

"Not my job. As long as Michael's in the running, I'll raise the money!" she pronounced confidently. "I love my work. This is the most exciting project I've ever worked on. It's so dynamic! Filled with risk—so much rests on forces beyond the fundraiser's control. The constant media pressure, reaction to charges by the opponent, the unknown and unforeseen crises. While I remain skeptical, especially in light of this mess, I've enjoyed seeing the political process close up. It's also helped me develop a different perspective on public service. Michael truly believes that he can make a difference."

Brenda nodded. "Jennifer, if he's the man of integrity you've been raving about, he'll survive. He may even come out of this more compassionate and a better public servant. In fact, it's not Michael that I'm so worried about. My concern is for you. When we started this insane adventure you were shaky on the question of whether or not you've fallen in love with Michael. Listening to you, I'm pretty sure that you have. If that's the case, then I'm curious how you'll handle him being a responsible, loving father."

Jennifer looked over at Brenda. She hadn't thought

that far ahead. It was all so premature but maybe Brenda had a point. "That's jumping a bit too far, Brenda." Then she remembered his kiss. Technically, they'd moved beyond a pure working relationship. It was all so confusing. She had no answers. Only tons of questions.

Brenda glanced over at Jennifer. She'd never seen her friend so conflicted. Who was she to doubt that Jennifer's feelings towards Michael were anything but real? While she didn't know Michael Wingate, she did know Jennifer Kelly. In the past, Jennifer had consciously kept men she dated at a distance. Well, Brenda thought, pleased with the notion, it seemed that Jennifer had met her match in Michael. And maybe, she thought, concerned and hopeful at the same time, Jennifer would be willing to open her heart to him.

"Bren, I honestly don't know. Is it possible that I won't know until I'm forced to deal with the facts?"

"Yes. It's very possible. Take your time. Right now you have a major fundraiser to help you stayed focused on your professional responsibilities.

Then Jennifer posed the question that was foremost on her mind. "What if I really am in love with Michael?"

"I don't know. You tell me."

"The thought is terrifying."

"Why is that, Jennifer? Are you afraid of facing his imperfections? Or is your love for him conditional? Be careful, Jennifer. There are enough women after Michael who want to be attached to him for all the wrong reasons. He doesn't need to get that from you, too. On the other hand, as close as you may think you are to him, it's only been a couple of months since you met the man. Give yourself time to get to know who he really is."

Jennifer alternated between clenching the steering wheel tightly and rubbing her long fingers against the leather covering as her thoughts warred in silence. She wasn't ready to think of Michael as a father or a man with a major attachment. Besides, she was still angry with him for not telling them that a potential crisis was brewing. He should have warned them...her, she really meant. It only made sense! How could she be expected to raise money in support of a candidate who couldn't be trusted? Reluctantly, she reminded herself that Michael was, after all, only a politician. And they had a habit of lying. She had made the mistake of letting her feelings for Michael get out of control. So, Jennifer realized, she had only herself to blame for the disappointment. "You're right, Bren. I don't know Michael all that well. I've got enough to do managing this last big gala."

"Jennifer, any regrets? I mean about working on the campaign. I know you were reluctant to get involved."

"No, at least not about working on the campaign. If you were to ask me if I regret getting involved personally, I'd have to think twice. You know I usually keep men at a distance. It's safer that way. I just can't figure out why it's so different with Michael."

"Well, for starters, he's fine, smart, charming, single, and in position to be a power broker in this country. You could do worse."

Jenny laughed with Brenda. "He is all of those things, but is he worth loving?"

"That, my dear friend, I suggest you continue to explore very carefully. He's not someone you should run from, at least not yet. Let him play this crisis out. It will give you both some time to sort out your feelings."

Jennifer smiled warmly. "You sound like my mother. You know patience isn't one of my strong suits. What do you suggest I do?"

"If it was me, I'd call him. Find out what time he's due into Hartford. Maybe you two could have dinner together, a quiet dinner, and just talk things out."

"Call him?" She mused. "Guess I could do that..."

"Just a thought." Brenda said quietly.

Jennifer dialed Michael on his cell and set it up. They talked only a few minutes, agreeing to have dinner together later that evening in Hartford.

They ordered room service. Michael, NY strip steak medium rare. Jennifer, grilled salmon. They sat adjacent to each other at the rectangular table in the dining area of his one-bedroom suite, their conversation strained.

Jennifer peered over the rim of her wine glass, her face void of animation. "I trusted you."

Michael shook his head regretfully. "And I hope you will again." Pausing, he measured his next words carefully, hoping they wouldn't inflame or cause more hurt. "There's no excuse, Jennifer. I was wrong and I'm sorry for hurting you." With pleading eyes, he held her close.

Jennifer remembered how her father had asked for her forgiveness too. It seemed to her right then that the men she loved asked too much from her. Then she thought about Sarah and their discussions on patience. She nodded for Michael to go on. She needed to hear more before she passed final judgement.

Michael filled in the details of the last month. He held nothing back, including the fact that he used the DNA testing as a way to hold off the media. "I didn't need to wait for a call from the lab. I sensed that Max was my son."

"Really? How so?"

"Because I know Daphne. I knew that she wouldn't lie about something so serious. Oh, I was good and angry that she'd waited so long to tell me. I felt cheated out of something so important, but it doesn't excuse me for not responding immediately."

"Because you procrastinated, she called the press?"

Michael looked up at Jennifer, shaking his head. "Daphne says she didn't call them."

"You believe her?"

"Yes." He stood and crossed the room. Head down, he kept his back to Jennifer. After a few minutes, he turned and walked slowly back across the room.

Michael took Jennifer's hand and helped her to her feet. Together they walked to the sofa. She dropped into a corner. Michael sank into the sofa, head bowed, chin nestled in his hands. In a controlled voice, he said, "Your friendship, your trust, is very important to me."

"It's important to me too," she admitted. "I agree that there's no sense in wasting time with regrets about the past." She thought of the years she'd spent on the West Coast alone and alienated from her parents. She folded her hands in her lap, signaling her willingness to listen.

Understanding the nonverbal sign, Michael smiled appreciatively. "Let me get something straight. Daphne is the mother of my son, not my girlfriend. I'm not in love with her and I don't believe that she's in love with me either. But we've been friends for years and we dated off and on in college.

He paused, remembering the day he'd first met Daphne. A laugh escaped from his lips. "We met the day Daphne came to interview me for the school paper. I was running for senior class president. She was soft-spoken, timid actually. She was a different person with the camera in her hand—confident, assertive, funny. The article was okay but the photos captured my mood and determination to win that election.

"Daphne left Harvard after graduation and went to NYU for graduate school to study photography and journalism. We stayed in touch by e-mail but I didn't see her again until I ran into her at a party last year. We left the party together." Lifting his head, his eyes locked with hers. "Daphne was leaving the next day for a long term assignment in Somalia. She was worried about how'd she react to tribal wars and the result of years of famine. We went to my place to talk but ended up making love. Max was conceived that night."

What about birth control? Jennifer wanted to ask but bit her lip instead. Her thoughts got stuck on his use of the term making love, wondering if he was being honest about not being in love with Daphne.

Not noticing the confused look on Jennifer's face, Michael proceeded to tell her more about the night he found out about Max.

Jennifer listened quietly. She felt like stopping him and explaining that nothing he was saying was shocking or hard to believe. She knew women like Daphne who took on the demands of single parenting without complaint or expectations of the baby's father. She also knew women who planned pregnancy even though they weren't married or in a committed relationship. Daphne had carried her independence to an extreme. But listening to Michael describe his conflict and the pain of not being included in the decisions surrounding his son's birth put a totally different spin on the situation.

"Yesterday I decided that it was time to go and see my son. On the way to Daphne's house I concocted all kinds of scenarios. I wanted her to be the villain. Needed to blame her and absolve myself, I guess. Then I thought about Max and the fact that his existence could screw up my life." He looked away, gathering strength before proceeding. "Sad, isn't it, to blame a baby? Anyway, I was nervous and scared but also suddenly very anxious to see my son." He met her somber eyes. "Until this happened, I'd taken being in control for granted. I'd always set my goals and met them pretty easily...no big hurdles...no major obstacles. Life was pretty...straightforward. I achieved whatever I set my mind on having. Women, grades, sports, even politics. While there has always been someone behind me cheering me on, the motivation came from within. The pressure came from me. I set the standard...loved the challenge...loved the success...the winning. Then I get this call telling me that I'm the father of a three-month-old baby boy." Michael paused, feeling the anger again. "I felt robbed of a most precious gift. Instead of choosing fatherhood, it was forced upon me." Unconsciously, Michael balled his hands into fists. "I'd always pictured it differently. Been very careful to preserve that moment so that it would be part of a package that included love and commitment."

"She used you," Jennifer said, convinced that Daphne had planned the pregnancy.

"Yes and no."

"How can you defend her?"

"Because I know her... Keeping her secret must have been torture. Then I saw her with Max. She's a warm, loving mother and Max is a happy, responsive baby." Michael looked at Jennifer, wondering how he was going to make her understand that he not only knew Daphne, he trusted her. His expression clouded. "I've known Daphne long enough to know that she's not a mean-spirited woman.

Besides, I'm as responsible for Max's existence as she is. I had a choice. I could have supported Daphne's fears that night without sleeping with her. I knew that we didn't love each other. Well, not that way. And it was shortsighted and irresponsible of me not to use protection. So, I can hardly blame Daphne or deny Max my love. Do you agree?"

A shiver ran through Jennifer. "I hear you, Michael. A child deserves two parents," she answered, thinking about her own half sister whom she might never meet.

"Yeah, well, I think that's why Daphne finally called me. Some of the realities of being a single mom hit her. Oh, that's not fair. She loves Max enough to want what's best for him. While it's not ideal, I'm going to see to it that Max has two active, involved parents."

"You're incredibly understanding and mature about this whole thing."

Michael smiled tenderly, his emotions close to the surface. "It's about time, don't you think? I was confused right up until the moment I set my eyes on my son. Then I held him in my arms and it all made sense."

She met his glazed look. "What now?"

"Now?"

"Yes, what now?"

Clearing his throat, he replied, "I made arrangements with Daphne to start spending time with Max. Eventually, I'll get joint custody."

He leaned towards her, his expression bold. "And I

want you. I have since that first night. Nothing's changed, Jenny,...nothing."

Studying him, she shook her head. "That's where you're wrong, Michael. Everything's changed."

"How so?" Michael was confused by the intensity he read in her eyes.

Jennifer stared back, wanting to explain that she felt closer to him now but more threatened by the obvious respect he still had for his son's mother. "We're different now."

Michael's smile softened. "Are we?" His eyes clung to hers, drinking in the desire he read in them.

Jennifer swallowed hard as she struggled with her need to touch him. "I guess this crisis has helped me see how important you've become to me."

"And you to me," he responded, his voice husky now.

"I don't know what I'm feeling exactly."

An easy, seductive smile spread across his lips. "Try me."

Licking her lips nervously, she plunged in deeper. "I've gotten very close to you over these past two months."

"Tell me more," he urged.

"Before we met I think I was jealous of the closeness you shared with my father and I was determined not to like you. But from that first moment I knew that dismissing you wasn't going to be so easy. As time went by my feelings shifted towards respect and admiration and, somewhere along the way, something else."

Pleased that they'd reached the same conclusion, he pressed. "Something else?"

Jennifer cracked a nervous smile as heat rushed to her cheeks. "Oh, stop making this so hard. You know what I mean. These past seven weeks, seeing you for twelve, fourteen hours a day...well, its gotten to the point where you're all I think about." She took a deep breath and prepared to go on, but Michael interrupted.

"In a purely professional sort of way?" he prompted, knowing she meant something else.

Looking down, she said softly, "No—not really."

"How so then?" he teased.

"It's natural, I guess, given the intimacy of our work environment and the intensity of the campaign." She eyed him cautiously. "Only problem is, I don't believe in sleeping with the boss," Jennifer finally said, praying that she'd kept it light enough that if he wasn't feeling the same way they could both laugh off the notion.

Michael smiled broadly. "And you won't be. You're technically a free woman. Didn't you tell me that we'll reach our goal tomorrow night?"

She smiled shyly, seeing the direction of his reasoning. "I did...and we will."

He chuckled. "Okay then. You're a success and certainly don't need a boss. So I resign, not as a candidate but as your boss." He inched towards her. "I know exactly what you're saying 'cause I've wanted you from the moment you flew into your father's office trying to be indignant about the fact that we were talking about you. I knew then, Jenny."

Eyes misting, she reached forward and stroked his cheek tenderly. "I see." She touched his lips softly. "If I'm honest I'd admit that I've wanted you since that first night, too."

"Why didn't you say something?" His smile deepened. "We've wasted time."

"No, not wasted. I've enjoyed every minute of our time together. I've never been teased so thoroughly nor anticipated lovemaking so completely."

Michael stood, pulling her up with him. "You sure it's all right with you?"

"I'm not sure of anything beyond this moment."

Michael held her eyes captive. "The only question that remains then is, what we're going to do about it?"

Her heart turned over as Michael's eyes dropped to her lips and lingered. "We'll have to be very careful. The last thing you need is more scandal."

"Yes, but just until after the election." Michael reached down and pulled her to him tightly, then kissed the top of her head, the tips of her ears, her forehead. He spoke, his voice close to a whisper, "Jennifer, I have nothing to offer you now."

Heart racing, she leaned closer, welcoming his kiss. "That makes us even."

His lips traveled down her face, covering every inch of its smooth, unblemished complexion with kisses until their lips met hungrily.

Jennifer's knees wobbled. She leaned against his strong male frame as he pressed his building erection into her thigh. "Michael, please," she moaned as his fingertips reached up to trace her taut nipples and full breasts.

"Please what?" he coaxed.

Jennifer shuddered. "Please make love to me."

"I intend to," he replied, pulling away unexpectedly.

Disappointed, Jennifer's eyes searched his eyes for answers.

Michael studied her for a moment, then gathered her hand in his. "Come with me, Jennifer. I want you naked."

He led her into the bedroom, sat on the edge of the bed and pulled Jennifer in front of him. "Take your clothes off, Jennifer."

Nodding, Jennifer eased slowly out of her jeans, lifted her T-shirt over her head, and released the clasps on her bra, dropping it to the floor without removing her eyes from his. Begging to be touched, she stood nearly naked before him, trembling as his eyes raked over her body.

"Beautiful," he murmured softly.

His fingers slipped into the black lace panties that separated her most private parts from him, easing them slowly over her hips.

Now she stood before him completely naked. Michael eased his body further onto the bed and spread his legs wide enough so that Jennifer could fit perfectly between them. "Let's take our time," he said, then reached up and pulled her to him and caressed her body until she felt weak with desire.

"Yes," she moaned, grasping his broad shoulders as a tormented groan escaped from her lips. "Michael, I can't..."

"Can't what?"

"Can't take it...," she moaned.

Jennifer rolled onto the middle of the king-size bed. Her eyes watched as Michael quickly undressed and moved his tall, magnificent body gracefully towards her. A shiver ran through her veins and her skin tingled with his first touch. His lips and fingertips explored, teased, and demanded her response. She arched her body to meet him and sank back as his fingers played with her marble hard nipples. His tongue caressed each swollen bud, then trailed down her belly. His fingers toyed with her clit, and dipped deep into her wetness.

A moan escaped from her full, moist lips, then a soft cry as he brought her to greater heights of ecstasy. She shuddered as her body throbbed in desperate longing. Remembering their pledge to take their time, she fell back, wanting to allow the pleasure to take over. Then, gasping in sweet agony, Jennifer pleaded for him to enter her.

Instead, Michael took her hand and guided it to his throbbing, hard organ.

It was her turn to love him now and she welcomed the chance to drive him insane with desire. Smiling mischievously, she pushed Michael back against the pillows and eased onto her elbow. With his shaft clamped in her cupped hand, she bent to taste him, teasing at first, then pulling him deep inside her mouth.

Groaning, Michael met her sweetness with a gentle thrusting of his hips as his fingers laced through her curls and kneaded her scalp. She enjoyed feeling him lose control as he surrendered completely. Ready to explode, she climbed on top of him and they rode in exquisite harmony until they cried out together in hot, raw satisfaction.

Michael rolled her over and slowed his movements, enjoying the sensuous lovemaking. He whispered words of love as his body rocked in smooth unison with hers.

She talked softly, proclaiming her love as she felt herself coming again.

Michael smiled, loving pleasing her and rode her with deep, long, slow strokes until they cried out together, satiated.

Jennifer collapsed in Michael's arms and let out a deep sigh. "I love you, Michael," she whispered as her body trembled repeatedly.

Michael wrapped his strong arms around her body and held her close. He kissed her shoulders and the back of her neck. "I love you, too, Jennifer." His fingers again toyed with her nipples, liking how they grew taunt under his touch. He felt his erection build again in response to the woman in his arms.

Jennifer scooted her body into Michael's curved, muscular frame. Her breathing quickened. Her hips rotated slowly.

Michael eased up on one elbow and whispered softly into her ear as he lifted her top leg and entered her again, "Oh Jenny, I do love you."

After hours of lovemaking, Jennifer and Michael lay in each other's arms and talked about politics and love until Michael drifted off to sleep.

Jennifer cradled Michael in her arms, watching him protectively. After his breathing evened out, she gently slipped her arm from under his head and eased out of bed. She couldn't risk exposure, so she dressed without waking him, then quietly left the suite, knowing that for now, at least, their lovemaking had to be kept a secret.

Nine

Jennifer stretched, smiling still from memories of a wonderful night of lovemaking. She wondered if Michael was awake yet and if he missed her.

She glanced over at the twin bed where Brenda lay still asleep. She knew her friend wouldn't approve of the fact that she'd had sex with Michael.

Jennifer grew serious as she remembered the hurdles they still had to climb. The gala was that night and by now news of Michael's paternity had certainly spread throughout the state. Desperate to hear how the story was being played out in Hartford, she turned on the TV just as photos of Michael flashed across the screen. Sitting up, Jennifer listened to the reporter's words with mounting trepidation. It was worse than she'd imagined.

"Michael Wingate's candidacy hits an all time low.

"Overnight polls show the popular senatorial candidate down by ten points. Stay tuned," the news anchor said as he shifted to a commercial break.

"Damn!" Jennifer cursed out loud. She barely had time to let the anxiety build before the anchor was back and recapping the devastating effect that the news had had on the overnight polls.

Jennifer sat up, alarmed even further when they showed a picture of Michael outside Daphne's house. The camera angle rolled in close as Michael leaned over and kissed Max while he was being held in Daphne's arms. The image of an intact family. A wave of insecurity hit her. The visual was so convincing. She cautioned herself not to go there. Fighting off the panic, she reminded herself that Michael had said that he loved her.

A voice inside signaled a warning. What if Michael's decision got swayed by voter response and demands? After all, marrying Daphne would make good political sense. At least that was one way you could interpret the rapid decline in the polls. Certainly it would be best for the baby.

Jennifer braced for the verbal attacks as the reporter took to the streets for public opinion. She knew that these would be gut reactions that would waver with the moment, but still they gave some indication on whether voters believed that Michael's campaign was irreparably damaged by the news.

The reporter interviewed men and women for a few unbearable seconds and their response was quite mixed.

Some felt that marrying his baby's mother offered the only chance Michael had to revive his campaign. Others were less judgmental, stating that they trusted Michael Wingate to act responsibly towards his child and that alone would determine his viability. Still others shrugged their shoulders as if they were without opinion or simply tired of the unreasonable expectations the public placed on public officials. "It happens," one man stated emphatically, swearing that it wouldn't affect perception for long.

Filled with uncertainty, Jennifer pulled the covers over her head and curled into a ball.

❦❦❦

Brenda peered over at the other twin bed. Seeing only a lumpy mass, she called out cautiously, "Jenny?"

Poking her head out from under the sheets, Jennifer stared blankly without uttering a word.

"Are you all right?"

She nodded, throwing off the covers. "You missed the TV coverage."

Brenda sat up in bed looking concerned. "That bad, huh?"

"Worse."

"Poor Michael," Brenda replied, thinking of his candidacy. She hardly knew the man but she liked him. "How did your meeting go last night?"

Frowning, Jennifer asked, "My meeting?"

"Yes, with Michael. Meeting, dinner, whatever…how did it go?"

"Oh, that…," she said, looking away. "It was fine."
Brenda eyed Jennifer skeptically. "So, you're not mad at him anymore?"

"Mad…no, I'm not mad."

"Jennifer, what's going on? You left here last night determined to find out what his intentions were and I wake up and you're hiding under the covers."

Caught, Jennifer met her friend's knowing look and shrugged. "Okay. We talked…"

"And?"

"Brenda, you know what happened!"

"No, I don't."

"We had a nice dinner and talked about the baby, his campaign and…"

"And?"

Jennifer sat up and wrapped the covers around her waist. A smile crossed her lips. "We had sex, okay?"

"Jennifer! You work for the man!"

Pulling her knees up to her chest, she rested her chin on her knees. "I know."

"Damn, girl. What were you thinking?"

"Only that I wanted to be with him. I can handle this, Brenda. Honestly."

"Jennifer, the man's in major trouble as it is. If it gets out that he's sleeping with a member of his staff…well."
She stumbled, flustered. "There'll be more hell to pay and

this time you'll be right in the middle of the madness."

"I have no intention of letting this get out."

"Really? And how are you going to play this off and act normal around a man you're having sex with?"

"I can do it!" Jennifer declared vehemently. "I have to do it. Trust me…," she repeated, her tone less sure.

"I hope so, Jennifer. 'Cause if you don't play this smart, someone's bound to find out and bust your cover."

Nodding, Jennifer grabbed her pillow and held it tight against her chest.

Brenda took a long, hard look at her friend and regretted her harsh words. "Sorry, I'm just worried about you, girl."

Throwing the pillow down, Jennifer hopped out of bed. "Everyone's worried about me…you, Michael…I can just imagine what my father's going to say. But I've survived worse trauma," she grumbled.

"I know. It's just that you've never been in love before. And this crisis with Michael is going to take time before it's resolved."

Jennifer spoke over her shoulder on her way to the bathroom, "Bren, do me a big favor and go get the newspapers."

"Sure." She started pulling on clothes.

Jennifer adjusted the water and stepped into the shower. With hot water pounding on her back, rational thoughts came to mind. Jennifer knew that shelving her personal feelings towards Michael until after the campaign was essential.

She turned her body so that the warm shower spray covered her face and throat, then turned again so that it beat against her weary back muscles. She felt soothed, healed. She eased her hands into the mass of curls that cascaded down to her shoulders and tilted her head backwards while she massaged her scalp with shampoo until it was squeaky clean. She applied conditioner and let it saturate her hair while she rinsed her body.

She'd just gotten out of the shower when she heard a door slamming. She wrapped the towel around her and called out through the closed bathroom door, "Brenda, is that you?"

"Yes, and you better get out here fast."

"Be right out." Jennifer quickly dried off and slipped into her bra and panties. She whisked open the door and found Brenda sitting on her bed so deeply engrossed in reading the newspaper that she didn't bother to look up.

"Brenda, what's wrong?"

Brenda looked up, face cloudy. "News isn't good."

"Let me see the papers." Jennifer reached for them.

"It's only the media's take on this, you know," Brenda said, hoping to prepare Jennifer.

"That bad, heh?" She took the stack of papers over to her bed and spread them out. *The Stamford Advocate, The Connecticut Times, Hartford Courant* and *Fairfield County*

Review all ran headlines dealing with Michael's paternity. She read them out loud.

"Senatorial Hopeful Michael Logan Admits Paternity," read the *Advocate*. Okay, she thought, that's fair. Reading on, she stared at the photo and caption under the picture of Michael, Daphne and their four-month-old son in the Fairfield paper. Its headlines read simply, "Can His Candidacy Survive?" Jennifer pushed that paper aside, again not overly concerned. She quickly read the story in the *Times*, the most reserved of the four papers. It ran the picture of six Connecticut residents and had quotes next to their pictures about Michael's chances. The overwhelming response was that everything depended on how Michael managed the situation, perhaps marrying his baby's mother or fighting for joint custody.

It took her only a few moments to find Michael's response in all the papers. "This is my personal business and I intend on acting responsibly." Then she wondered aloud, "What the hell does that mean?" Both as a voter and as the woman who was in love with him, she hated the vagueness of his response.

Annoyed that she was already overreacting, Brenda reminded Jennifer of her pledge. "Jennifer, calm down. You knew that this was coming."

Jennifer glowered at Brenda before taking her advice. She thought about tossing the pile of papers in the trash and moving on, but then her eyes settled on one tabloid headline. Spooked, she sank onto her bed, her eyes still fixed on the bold, declarative headline, "Michael Logan Wingate, Democratic Nominee for U.S. Senate, to Marry Mother of His Son."

Ten

It was a hectic day without a single word from Michael. Jennifer made a final sweep through the ballroom, feeling buoyed by the brightly-colored balloons that adorned the room. The tables were set with tall, champagne-colored candles and centerpieces of tight clusters of peach and yellow roses mixed with orange daylilies. Diane Reeves was on the stage with her jazz combo rehearsing the Luther Henderson rendition of Duke Ellington's "Sophisticated Lady."

Satisfied that the stage was set for a successful evening, she headed back to her room to dress. She was due in Michael's suite for a staff meeting in an hour.

On the way out, she stopped at a stack of programs that were in a corner waiting for the volunteers to distribute them to the tables. Grabbing several at once, she shattered the nail on the middle finger of her left hand. It happened so quickly that a stinging pain shot through her hand. She studied the damage. Rushing off, she dropped by the hotel gift shop and picked up a package of Lee press-on nails.

Back in her room, Jennifer attempted to mend her broken nail while she waited for Brenda to emerge from the bathroom. She cut the nail to the right length, applied the glue and proceeded to apply it to the tip of the broken nail. "Damn!" she swore loudly as it slid onto the carpet.

Brenda rushed from behind the closed bathroom door wrapped in a white towel. "Jennifer, what's the matter?" Jennifer seemed to be crawling around on the floor.

Spotting the nail, she glanced up at Brenda in embarrassment. "These damn fake nails. They're so hard to apply."

"Which is why you should have gone and gotten a proper manicure."

"I did, but I broke a nail a few minutes ago. Bren, I need your help," she moaned, extending her hand with the plastic nail in her palm. "I'm due up in Michael's room in thirty minutes for a staff meeting."

Exchanging the towel for a short silk robe, Brenda shook her head and tried not to laugh. She could tell that her girlfriend was truly distraught and not in the mood to see the humor in her present situation. "You know this is trifling, don't you, girl? I mean, I've never seen you let a man get you this confused. What exactly is your problem now?"

"You saw that picture of him kissing Daphne!" Jennifer's voice rose an octave as she spoke.

Hands on her hips, Brenda replied. "Yeah, and…?"

"Well, what do you make of it? Looks like they're pretty connected, right? Why hasn't he called."

"Probably 'cause he's concerned with salvaging his image," Brenda reminded her. "Let's stop the drama, Jenny. You know the man's fighting for his career and he knows that you have the fundraiser under control."

"Yeah, well, he still should have checked in with me. I mean, for God's sake, this paternity business affects everything, including the gala. We could have had massive declines for all he knows. But no, instead of a courtesy call, he has Maxine call me to a meeting in his suite like nothing's happened."

"Jennifer, you're confusing the issues again."

"Maybe I am," she conceded. "But he knows I'm worried half out of my mind!"

Pulling up the other chair, Brenda took the nail from Jennifer and began the mending process. She peered at her friend and frowned. "Apart from being worried about the campaign, how are you really feeling?"

Jennifer sighed. "Scared. Mad."

Brenda smiled. "So I see. But at whom?"

"Myself, for letting this get to me. I thought I could handle whatever came next."

"Well, you were expecting too much of yourself, as

usual, and besides, you know how insecure women feel the day after the first time with a man."

"Brenda, it's not like I'm a virgin…"

"Yeah, but this is the first time you've been in love, Jennifer."

"Maybe."

"Maybe nothing. I've known every detail of your past relationships and you've never fallen this hard." She eyed her friend cautiously. "Just take it slow. That's all I ask."

"Take it slow…isn't it a bit too late for that advice?"

"From this point on, Jennifer. Especially given all that's happened with Michael and this other woman. The press will be watching him like a hawk. Besides, until Michael gets his campaign and personal life back on track, he has little to offer you."

Jennifer cracked a smile, remembering the conversation she'd had with Michael the night before. "He tried to tell me that last night. Brenda, how am I going to go up to his suite and pretend like nothing's bothering me?"

Brenda rubbed her friend's hands and spoke softly. "You'll do it because you have a job to complete. After that, you can decide what you want to do about your feelings towards Michael. Gala, first. Love, second. It's just that simple."

Jennifer touched Brenda's cheek. "You're a good friend, Bren. Thanks for not saying I-told-you-so."

"Go, your shower awaits. And when you see Mr. Wingate, play it off as if nothing happened last night. Act like a loyal, dedicated member of the staff! Not like the woman he had sex with last night."

Laughing, Jennifer jumped up and accepted her marching orders like a good soldier.

Thirty minutes later, dressed all in black and looking sophisticated and calm, Jennifer knocked on the door to Michael's suite. When a somber-looking Jerry opened the door, she stepped inside into a crowded suite.

Michael was on the couch reviewing his remarks with Maxine. His eyes lifted as Jennifer crossed the room. He stopped speaking mid-sentence. "Jennifer, come here." His hands opened in a gesture of welcome, and his eyes were soft and appreciative.

Praying that her legs wouldn't betray her, Jennifer walked across the room and took a seat opposite Michael. She tried to keep her mind focused on the political jargon that passed between the staffers, but hard as she tried, her thoughts kept wandering. One minute Michael Wingate was a politician. The next moment he was her lover. Fighting back an inappropriate grin, she forced her mind back to the conversation just in time to hear Michael's question.

"How are things downstairs?"

She stared blankly for a moment, then answered briefly. "The ballroom looks great. The program is set.

We're sold out. Now let's just hope our guests show up."

His true supporters would be there to cheer him on and restate their belief in his ability to win. Others would come if for no other reason than to be nosey. Yet she was plagued by doubts. Playing the role of a detached professional fundraiser was harder than she'd imagined. Jennifer just wanted the evening to be over with quickly.

"They'll come," Michael said, offering Jennifer a reassuring smile. "Thanks, Jennifer. I know the news of my paternity put an extra stress on you all, but I can't begin to tell you how much I appreciate your support."

Her eyes drifted to the coffee table. The tabloid was laid open to the article that claimed Michael would wed his son's mother. Her muscles tensed involuntarily.

They'd probably discussed the article when she wasn't around. Michael would have planned it that way to avoid causing her further pain. She toyed nervously with her hands and kept her eyes down. A small voice inside reminded her to remain calm, nonjudgmental, slightly aloft. "The press are swarming around," she said, looking at Maxine and Jerry.

Michael, ignoring the fact that Jennifer had directed her concerns to his staff, said, "We talked about how to handle the press before you arrived, Jennifer."

She swung her head around, suddenly furious that he hadn't called her before the meeting to talk privately about his plans. "Would one of you please fill me in?" She glared at Michael.

"I have no intention of discussing my paternity at the gala," Michael barked. Seeing her flinch, he immediately regretted his tone. Softening a bit, he explained the strategy that they'd worked out. "After the dinner, I'll meet with the press. Jerry's prepared a statement which you all should familiarize yourselves with before we go downstairs."

"What do we say when we're asked about the range of solutions suggested in the various articles?" she asked, thinking only of the one that claimed he intended on marrying Daphne.

"You say nothing. It's my personal concern. I have no intention of allowing this to interrupt the gala or my campaign. I'm going all the way and I intend to win." Michael held her eyes steady. "Believe me, I know it's a lot to process. I'm dealing with the news as best I can and still keep this campaign moving forward. I'm not asking you to make any excuses for me. Are you still with me?" Michael searched Jennifer's face and found her expression to be noncommittal.

Jerry spoke up. "Michael, you know we believe in you. This news hasn't changed that in the least."

"Thank you, Jerry. Is there anyone who wants out?" Michael asked, still looking at Jennifer.

Desperate to escape, she stood without dignifying Michael's question with an answer. "I have to get back downstairs. What time will you be joining us?"

"What time is the program scheduled to begin?"

"The reception is from six-thirty to seven-thirty.

Dinner will be served at eight, the program begins at eight-thirty."

Jerry jumped in. "We'll bring Michael down at seven. He wants to mingle a bit before the program begins."

"I'll alert security."

"They're already alerted, Jennifer," Jerry said.

"Fine. Then I'll see you downstairs." Jennifer quickly exited the suite without looking in Michael's direction.

❧❧❧

By the time Jennifer slipped her plastic key into the slot, it was well after midnight. Peering into the darkened room, she realized that Brenda was already asleep. Exhausted, Jennifer kept the lights off while she stripped. Her black silk crepe dress fell in a pile at her feet. Slipping out of the jeweled black high heels, she stepped over the pile and headed for the bathroom to remove her makeup.

She stared into the mirror, surprised by the dull and sad gray eyes that peered back at her. The emotional flip-flop of the past forty-eight hours had taken its toll.

Creaming off her makeup, she thought about the gala. It had been the success she'd anticipated but not without moments of drama. Michael had tried to be charming, but his body was stiff, his comments terse, his smile tight. Most of the tables were filled but there were plenty of empty seats. The press conference was short and to the point. Michael made his statement, refusing to elaborate on his plans other than to say he intended on being an active father.

Though she'd acted professionally, the evening was even more difficult for her to manage than she'd anticipated. Truth was their lovemaking had left her fraught with anxiety. The sex had changed their ease with each other and their expectations. As if that weren't enough, the tabloids had done their number on her. Assigning some of her doubts to exhaustion, Jennifer slipped on a nightgown. If she were honest with herself, it hadn't been easy from the start to work so intimately with a man she found so attractive. She'd entered the campaign with mixed motivations, though she told everyone that it was the allure of working on a national campaign that had changed her mind. But in fact it was the thought of working side-by-side twelve to fourteen hours a day with Michael that had really clenched the deal.

She'd liked his passion, strong sense of self, clear vision, confidence and the fact that Michael wouldn't allow himself to be controlled by anyone, not even her father. What she hadn't counted on was falling in love. And now that deep, unfamiliar emotion had become a distraction and a source of pain that she was going to have to control better. There were only five weeks left to the campaign. Actually four weeks and five days to stay focused on winning. She could play the game for thirty-six more days. But there would be no more intimate dinners after a long day or supportive chats in her office. And no more sex.

Jennifer knew what she had to do to keep her feelings about Michael at bay. She'd allowed the search for her sister to drop to second place behind Michael's campaign. Now that her final major fundraiser was over, she'd jump back into the process and help her father find her sister. She had to bring her family together whether or not Michael won the election, married the mother of his son or gave up the senatorial race or moved to Ghana. Finding her sister, she reminded herself, was critical to her happiness. That was her mission. Michael's campaign was her job.

As soon as the campaign was over and after she met her sister, maybe she should go back to L.A. for a while. She tried to bring up visions of the life she'd return to: the rugged Pacific Coast shoreline with bluish-gray waves pounding the rocks, the seagull and sandpiper conventions along the water's edge, the warm sun, but thoughts of Michael filtered through.

Tears clouded her vision. The thought of leaving Michael was painful. Sighing, Jennifer willed her mind to stop going beyond the moment. Sleep was the best remedy for the nagging despair. In the morning, she'd be stronger, wiser.

Jennifer opened the bathroom door, took a minute for her eyes to adjust to the darkness, then ventured quietly into the bedroom. "Damn," she muttered when she bumped into the edge of the dresser.

Brenda groaned as she turned over and switched on the lamp by her bed. "Does that help?"

"Sorry, didn't mean to wake you," Jennifer apologized.

"You didn't. Your boss did," she yawned.

"Michael?"

"Do you have another boss?"

"Look, this is not the time to be amusing. What did he want?"

"Wants you to come up to his suite for a post mortem…or whatever they call it. The gala, by the way, was da bomb."

She felt her temper rise at the thought of facing the group again tonight. "The last thing I need right now is a meeting with the group."

"What?" Brenda asked, half asleep and confused by Jennifer's tone.

"Oh, never mind. How long ago did he call?"

"Just a few minutes. You were in the bathroom."

"Did you tell him I was here?"

"I did. Why? What's up? Did you two have words?"

"No. I'm just tired and don't feel like rehashing the evening with Jerry and Maxine."

"Well, my friend, looks like that's exactly what you'll be doing. But I'm going back to sleep. Turn off the light when you leave, okay?"

"I'm not going anywhere," Jennifer murmured as she slid into bed.

Eleven

Michael woke up alone and rolled over onto the side of the bed. He'd hoped that Jennifer would be beside him, but she hadn't even called him back. Trying to be sensitive, he'd accepted her decision not to come to him.

Reaching for the remote, he flipped on the television and adjusted the volume to an audible hum. The local newscasters announced a commercial break as they headed into the second half of the early morning show. Michael walked over to the heavy velveteen drapes, pulling them back to let the early light of sunrise filter into the room. He loved morning, especially during daylight savings time when six-thirty didn't look like the middle of the night. He turned just in time to see his face plastered across the screen. The reporter was on the streets of downtown

Hartford doing interviews. It was night, so he assumed the interviews had taken place sometime while they were at the gala. Yes, in fact the reporter mentioned something to that effect. Anyway, strangers offered comments on whether he should marry the mother of his baby as if they really knew him and understood his choices. Michael froze, stunned by the blatant, unforgiving invasion into his private matters. Then the reporter moved on, stating that according to the overnight tracking polls, Michael Wingate's lead had taken a major hit. He concluded by posing the question of why the Wingate campaign hadn't put this story out themselves and controlled the content better.

Pulse racing, Michael retrieved the morning papers from outside the door. There prominently displayed on the front cover of the New Haven Review was a photo of him kissing Daphne on the lips. That blew his anger over the top. Throwing down the paper without reading beyond the photo caption, Michael dialed Jerry's room and barked into the phone.

"Jerry, why the hell didn't you call me earlier! Get up here now," he shouted. "And get Maxine up here, too." Slamming the phone down, he slipped into a jogging suit and read the papers until his team arrived.

He resented the fact that the papers were filled with public opinion about what his responsibility was to the baby's mother. If he followed public opinion, marriage was his next step. But then, the public hadn't heard his side of the story and had only the photo of him kissing Daphne to go by. He realized that the one-sided story was a distraction at best and a potential killer at worst. He paced, thinking how best to quickly move the voters away from his private life and back onto the differences between him and his opponent on key issues.

His thoughts turned back to the photo. It had to be doctored. He had barely even kissed Daphne in the course of lovemaking, much less the day he went to see Max. Only he and Daphne knew that they weren't in love. He'd been very careful not to give her the false impression that he was interested in marriage. Even the day he went to see her, he hadn't promised her anything other than a call from his lawyer. Joint custody did not translate into a marriage proposal and he now knew that he had to make that clear to the public. He'd hoped that he wouldn't have to go into any more detail than a basic acknowledgment of his paternity.

An image of Jennifer's trusting eyes flashed in his head. He gritted his teeth. Damned if she'll trust me again, he thought. He considered his options as he checked the time. Not wanting to blow it twice with Jennifer, he rushed to the phone and dialed her room.

It rang five times before the operator cut in.

"Mr. Wingate, may I help you?"

"I'm trying to reach Jennifer Kelly in room 1414."

"I'm sorry, Mr. Wingate, but Miss Kelly checked out."

"Checked out!" he shouted into the phone, then immediately apologized. "I'm sorry. I didn't mean to yell.

Thank you."

Michael hung up and dialed her cell number. It rang and rang until her voice mail picked up.

"You've reached Jennifer Kelly's voice mail. Please leave a message."

"Jennifer, it's Michael. Call me on my cell phone as soon as you get this message. Jennifer, please..." He hesitated, knowing that a voice mail message wasn't the place to apologize or plead his case. "Well, anyway, I'll be leaving here in an hour and heading to the office. Meet me there later. We need to talk."

The doorbell rang just as he was hanging up the phone. Michael slung open the door. "Morning, Jerry, Maxine. Come in." Feeling seriously distracted but less angry, he waved them in.

"I assumed we would need legal advice so Jackson is on his way over. He should be here in ten minutes," Jerry said. Maxine went to the phone and ordered coffee and a basket of baked goods. "You've got your cell phone, right, Michael?"

"Yes, why?"

"Maybe I should have the front desk hold all other calls until we've had a chance to talk."

"You're right, Maxine," Jerry said, nodding in agreement. "Michael, is that okay with you?"

Michael nodded yes.

Maxine was already dialing the front desk. "Good morning. This is Maxine Washington, Michael Wingate's press secretary. Please hold all calls to Mr. Wingate's suite." She paused. "That's right. We'll notify you when it's okay to ring the suite. Thank you." Returning to the sofa, she joined in the discussion.

Maxine took over leadership of the meeting. "While we're waiting for Jackson, let's look at the key points from each of the papers. Michael, we'll need you to address each one as openly and honestly as you can. Then after we've received advice from legal, we'll proceed accordingly. Does that work for you guys?"

Michael and Jerry nodded in agreement.

Maxine continued, "I've summarized the key points in each of the papers." She handed Michael and Jerry a copy of her report.

Michael looked up. "Maxine, tell me something. The tabloids ran a photo of me kissing Daphne. Max is in the picture so it makes it look like we're already a family. Now I know I didn't kiss Daphne when I visited her, so where'd they get the photo?"

"Good point, Michael. And that's the kind of detail we need to deal with." Picking up the article in question, she asked, "This wasn't taken on your visit?"

"No. I'm absolutely positive."

"Then the picture probably has been tampered with. You know computers can do just about anything these days. That's a good question for legal."

"Michael, the *Connecticut Times* coverage is pretty benign. They talked with potential voters and got a cross section of answers. It seems fair, non-biased reporting. Do you agree?" Maxine asked, thankful that at least the paper with the largest circulation had refrained from drawing conclusions.

"I do," Michael voiced from behind fisted hands that supported his chin.

They talked on for ten minutes, then Jerry made a suggestion. "Michael, I think that the more contrite and sincere you come off the better. We need to put this distraction to rest quickly before it sinks too deeply into the hearts and minds of the voters. I say we hold a press conference this morning. Issue a statement. Answer questions unequivocally. Stick to your plan to deal responsibly without dignifying the media's need to control your actions. Make it clear that you take your role as a parent very seriously. Clarify what you can for them, and then move on to your policies and drive this campaign back to the major issues," Jerry directed.

Maxine nodded, then asked Michael a few questions. "The child support issue—can you prove that you've sent her child support? You're not behind in your payments, are you?"

Agitated, Michael slammed his fist on the table. "How can I be behind? The baby's only four-months-old. I've known of his existence for three-and-a-half weeks." Shaking his head, he apologized for his outburst. "I've sent her money, but Jackson's still working on the legal agreement." Michael stood, frustrated. He paced for a few minutes, then turned back around facing Maxine. "Where the hell is Jackson? Get him on his cell and find out where he is!" Michael demanded.

While Jerry moved from the table to phone Jackson, Maxine pushed forward. "Sorry, Michael, but I've got one more question." She knew the press were going to grill her.

"What are your plans?"

He stopped pacing and stood next to Maxine. Their eyes met. "I want joint custody."

"Do you expect Daphne to object?"

"No."

"Why is that?"

"She'll accept the joint custody arrangement because it's in Max's best interest," he stated emphatically.

"So you have no intention of marrying her?"

"None whatsoever!"

"Does she know that?"

"I made it perfectly clear."

"Let's hope so." Maxine hesitated. "Michael, excuse me for prying, but is there someone else?"

"No one that I care to talk about."

"I see." Maxine had noticed the way he looked at Jennifer and suspected that they were involved with each other more than they let on. It was not unusual for campaign staff members to form close friendships. The intensity of the work contributed to the ease of bonding. "Voters prefer stable married men. You knew that when you chose to run. This revelation of an out-of-wedlock pregnancy compounds their concerns about you being single. The fact that you didn't even see the baby until he was four-months-old will fuel their fears further. Never mind that you didn't know of his existence until a month ago, you'll still be considered reckless. So, I agree with Jerry. You need to directly address the issues raised. If you don't, people will continue to speculate and the story will grow legs," Maxine said as she stood and poured herself another cup of coffee.

Michael joined her, their eyes meeting briefly. "Okay," he said quietly.

Jerry returned from the phones and helped himself to coffee and a bagel. "Jackson will be here any minute."

Sipping coffee, they continued to talk strategy and get legal advice once Jackson arrived. Not wanting to postpone the inevitable any longer, Michael finally gave the go-ahead. "Maxine, arrange a press conference for ten. Let's do it in the hotel. Get a conference room."

Maxine rushed out to set up the press conference while the three men remained behind to flesh out the remaining details of his message. When they concluded, Michael said, "Thank you all for your support. If you'll excuse me, I'm going to call Moses and get his input on this as well."

🐝🦋🐝

By ten, Michael was holding court to a dozen print, radio, and TV journalists. "Thank you all for coming today. As you can imagine, this is a very difficult time. A few days ago I met my baby and discussed plans for his upbringing with his mother. While we are in the process of defining the terms, we are in agreement that Max needs two parents. He will have that. Daphne Wade and I have been friends since college. We'll continue to be friends. For my son's sake, I'm appealing to the media to give us the privacy we need to establish a routine and joint custody arrangement that will give Max the love and support he deserves."

The members of the press that were present were gentle in their attack, giving Michael the hope that they'd be fair in their reporting as well. By ten-forty-five, reporters rushed out to file their pieces in time for the midday news. A few of the print journalists, who had longer lead-time, hung around to get more information. As the last of the reporters left, Michael gave his crew marching orders before heading down to his office in Stamford. As he rose to leave, he studied the two individuals who had helped him get so close to being the favorite candidate. He sadly apologized for the mess he'd made of things.

Jerry swallowed hard. "Hey, Michael, there's no need to apologize. At least not to me."

"Me either," Maxine chimed in.

Michael smiled. "I hear you."

Maxine gathered her things and headed towards the door. "I'd better head on down to the office."

Michael watched her leave. "Thanks, Maxine."

Turning around, she said, "You're welcome, Michael. I've already sent an e-mail to all the staff reminding them not to speak to the press. I'll handle the press calls personally when I reach the office. Do you want to speak directly to the staff?"

"Yes, please call for a staff meeting at three. Jerry and I will head down just as soon as we finish up here."

Maxine waved goodbye and left to hold down the fort until Michael made it into the office. While she was sorry to see Michael have to endure the invasion into his private life, she also felt certain that he would be able to turn it around in his favor. In fact, it would give him the opportunity to demonstrate his personal commitment to many of the family values he'd so strongly espoused in his campaign speeches. No, she predicted, Michael Wingate would come out looking strong. The voters would admire how he'd handled a personal crisis without allowing it to deter him from his mission to serve them. Besides, she chuckled, he was the most charming man she'd ever met. If his honesty didn't convince the woman voters to stick with him, his charm would win them over. As for the men, she didn't see any real problem. Not many of them could stand up to the test any better than Michael. In fact, he was far superior to most. No, she smiled as she quickened her step, they'd have to work hard but it could be done. And then she'd move to Washington, D.C.

Jennifer arrived at her office just before noon. She'd gotten Michael's voice mail but had not called him back yet. She shut her office door and slumped into her chair, needing time to think. Michael was due in soon and she knew that he'd demand an explanation.

Her hands trembled slightly as she made notes. There were so many things to follow up on after a big event. Thankfully it wasn't a particularly difficult task. There was no strategizing necessary, just a matter of making a list and checking off the items as they were completed.

Classical music played softly in the background. It helped her stay focused as she wrote down the names of all those who had to be thanked. The next five weeks would pass quickly, then she'd fly immediately back to LA. And then... Well, she'd deal with the future as it happened. Right now people had to be thanked.

List completed, she stood and walked to the window. She saw others walking to and from the building. She got so caught up in imagining the lives of others that she barely heard the soft knock on her door. "Come in," she called out without turning around.

"Hello," he said from a distance.

Jennifer froze. She slowly turned her stiff body in the direction of the familiar voice. Her dull eyes lifted to met his troubled gaze. "Michael," she said softly.

Michael shoved his hands into his pockets. "May I come in?" he asked. "I tried to reach you all morning. Didn't you get any of my messages?"

"I did," she replied without apology.

"Then why didn't you call me back?"

She stared at Michael blankly. "I knew I'd see you today."

"And?"

"And we would debrief then. That's all."

"I wanted to thank you."

"And you did, several times during the course of the gala."

"Yeah, but I wanted to thank you in private."

"Not at midnight, Michael." She cut him a cool look.

"And then I called your room and you'd already checked out."

"I needed to drop Brenda off and get here to send out thank you letters."

Closing the door, he stepped inside cautiously, one hand resting on the door handle. "That's it?"

"That's what?"

"Jennifer, stop playing games! By now you must have read the papers, heard the gossip, formed some impressions…"

"I'm not playing games, Michael. I'm just trying to deal with everything. You know, stay focused. Help you win this election."

Michael flicked the lock on the door and walked towards Jennifer, smiling. "So, you're staying on?"

"Absolutely!"

"Oh, I was afraid you'd be finishing up the details from

last night then be on the next plane back to L.A."

Jennifer laughed, choosing a position of strength. "Shows you how little you know me."

"I intend on getting to know you better," he challenged, so close now that she could smell his cologne. "We had a press conference this morning at the hotel. I felt that it was important to clarify my position about Max and his mother."

"I see. What did you tell them?"

"That I intend to work out a joint custody arrangement with Daphne but that we have no marriage plans." Jennifer wondered if her relief showed. "How did they respond?"

"They pressed me on why it took me so long to acknowledge my son and to bring the issue public. I responded by saying that I was dealing with the news as best as I could. I also talked about the steps I took towards acceptance and the bonding that occurred when I saw Max for the first time."

"How do you feel now?" she asked.

"Better, actually. What about you?"

"I'm fine, Michael."

"I enjoyed the other night," he added, his eyes roving over her body.

"Look, Michael, the other night…shouldn't have happened." Stumbling a bit over her words, she grabbed onto the edge of her desk for support.

Michael took another step to bridge the gap. He was a

bit taken off guard. "We love each other, Jennifer. This crisis with Max will pass and then we can get on with our future."

"Future? Michael, let's stay in the present. You've got four-and-a half weeks to reclaim your lead in this campaign. That's where all our energy needs to be."

Michael shook his head and pressed forward. He wasn't letting her get away. "Yeah, well, once things settle down some we'll get away from here."

Jennifer bit her lip, not wanting her determination to falter. She silently renewed her vow to keep her distance, for now at least. "We'll see about that, Mr. Wingate. After you've won the election, that is."

"I intend on winning, Miss Kelly." Michael spoke with the certainty of a man who was accustomed to winning. "And I'm not just talking about the election," he added.

"We'll see about that, too." She felt steady, confident, until he grabbed her to him. Then she could feel her heart hammering against his.

Holding her head gently between his massive hands, he studied her face, wanting desperately to make love to her right then. "It's not going to be easy, you know."

Jennifer smiled warmly. "It hasn't been easy. I believe in you, Michael. You'll pull through this. I just know it," she said, pulling away and taking a step backwards.

His smile broadened, encouraged by her faith in him. "I hope you're right." Michael checked his watch. "I better get going. We have a staff meeting in thirty minutes and I need to get an update from Jerry and Maxine before facing the group." He started to walk out, then turned back to Jennifer looking concerned. "Sure you're all right?"

"Michael, I'm fine. Please don't worry about me."

"What's on your agenda for today?"

"I pick your mother up at five-thirty. She speaks at a dinner given by the Girl Friends." Jennifer paused, smiling up at him. "She's great, Michael. So comfortable in groups—just the right mixture of intimacy and distance. The women love her."

"She's enjoying working with you too. Sings your praises daily. In fact, I believe she's matchmaking." He chuckled. "I'm so tempted to tell her that it's already a done deal."

"Oh, really?" she teased.

"Well, if I have my way, that is."

Turning the doorknob, he looked her over one last time. "Jennifer?"

"Yes, Michael."

"Thanks."

"For?"

"Sticking with me."

"Oh, you're welcome."

As Michael exited, closing the door behind him, Jennifer let out a sigh. She walked back to her desk and picked up the phone. She needed to confide in someone.

Sarah answered the phone on the third ring. She'd stayed home from work, sickened by the news of Michael's paternity. She'd been disappointed and angry. Moses' reaction hadn't helped matters. He'd seemed concerned only about how the news would affect Michael's campaign. He'd also failed to see the irony in mentor and mentee both being exposed for fathering children out-of-wedlock. They'd argued and Moses had left angry, leaving Sarah distraught and conflicted. "Jennifer, how are you?"

"I'm fine, Mom. Have you been following the story about Michael's baby?"

"Oh, course. I'm so sorry, Jennifer."

"Yeah, me too. But I'm not sure who I feel sorry for, Mom. Michael feels confident that he'll survive. It seems that Daphne's a strong woman. So she'll be all right. But it's a shame that Max will have to live with this scandal all of his life."

"I tried to talk with your father about it this morning but we just ended up arguing. Men see paternity different from the way we do. They think that paying the expenses and visiting a child will make up for their not being a full time father."

"I'm not sure if that's fair, Mom. I know that this brings up your feelings towards Dad but Michael seems genuinely upset and determined to make things right for Max.

"He's asked Daphne for joint custody."

"Don't make excuses for him, Jenny. He should have

told us as soon as he found out. Then we could have been helpful." She sighed. "I've been so hurt that I haven't even tried to reach out to him. But I will. I'll also try not to take out my anger at your father on Michael. I know that the circumstances are quite different."

"I hear you. I'm hurting myself. That's part of why I called you."

"You're in this deeper than you've let on, aren't you?"

"Yes. And I need your advice."

"Just how involved are you, Jenny?"

"I'm in love with Michael, Mom. For a while, I just thought it was the intensity of our working relationship, but now I know better."

"I see. Does he feel the same way?"

"He says he does but who knows how things will turn out now."

"I'm assuming that you've had sex with him."

"We did. The other night."

"After you heard about the baby?"

"Yes."

"Jenny, Michael has enough problems right now. He can't possibly know how he really feels about you. Your timing was not well thought out."

"I guess that's what scares me. I don't want to complicate his life any more than it already is."

Sarah softened. "Jennifer, I'm not going to lecture you. You're an adult. I'm sure that Michael thinks that he's in love, too, but Jennifer, this baby situation changes a whole lot of things."

"I know, Mom. But what should I do?"

"Keep your distance. Stay focused on work and away from Michael. Let him get through this campaign. That's all he can handle right now. Give him some time."

"I came to that same conclusion. Thanks, Mom. I know you're right. I've got to go to staff meeting. See you tonight."

"Be careful, Jennifer, not to let your feelings get in the way."

She smiled, thinking it was a bit late for that advice. "I'll be careful, Mom."

Twelve

Jennifer poked her head into Maxine's office, hoping to pick up the guest list for Michael's election night party. Helping to coordinate what they hoped would turn out to be a victory celebration would be her final act on behalf of the campaign.

The last four weeks of the campaign had flown by. She'd seen Michael every day but not alone. He'd visited two or three cities a day, talking to thousands of potential voters. He'd pulled back up in the polls and winning looked possible once again.

"Good morning, Maxine."

"Jennifer, I was just finishing up this list. Come in. It will only take me a few more minutes."

"I thought you'd completed that list yesterday,"

Jennifer said, even though she knew that because of the political nature of a guest list it was never really complete.

"Me too. No, Michael called me late last night with some additions."

"That doesn't surprise me."

While Maxine entered the last of the names into the computer, Jennifer chatted on, not caring whether Maxine was paying attention. "The Marriott is going out of their way to accommodate us. They must share our belief that Michael's going to win. Anyway, they're renaming the presidential suite as the senator's suite. It's a two-bedroom, two-bath suite with a large living room, a decent size dinning room with a table that seats eight, and a small kitchen. There's a big screen TV in the living room so Michael can have people up to watch the election returns. Did he say who he wants in the suite?"

Maxine hit print and looked up. "Yes. There's a separate list for that." While the list was printing, the two women continued talking. "Jennifer, are you still heading back to L.A.?"

"I'm not sure. Why?"

"Just wondering. Has Michael talked with you about your plans?"

"Not recently. Why do you ask?"

"I don't know. Michael's been talking about who he intends to keep on—you know, if he wins."

Curious, she asked, "Was my name mentioned?"

"No. It wasn't. That surprised me but then I figured

you must have told him that you weren't staying. Do you have another project waiting for you in L.A.?"

"I've got a few options, but I haven't made any decisions yet."

"What do you want to do, Jenny?"

"I'm not even sure, Maxine."

"So why not come to D.C. with us?"

"Because I live in L.A.—remember?"

"I understand but you're really an East Coast girl so why not D.C.?" Maxine persisted. She wondered if Jennifer's return to L.A. had something to do with a man other than Michael. Why else would she reject an opportunity to work on the hill?

Jennifer looked at Maxine, not wanting her to know that she'd crossed the line and been intimate with the boss. If she went, it would be as Michael's wife, not as a member of his staff. "I'll come back East someday," she said, already feeling like an outsider. Michael was making plans, personal and professional. She wondered where she fit in.

Maxine studied the turmoil in Jennifer's face.

Jennifer twirled her bold silver thumb ring around and around, her head bent low. She was so absorbed in her thoughts that she was hardly aware of Maxine or the silence that separated them.

Maxine retrieved the list from the printer and handed Jennifer the ten-page alphabetical document. "Jennifer."

Jennifer looked up and met Maxine's questioning eyes. "Yes."

"After you've had a chance to review this, let's talk. I'm sure you'll find that I've missed some folks."

"Fine. Thanks Maxine." It was her job to cross-reference the list Maxine prepared with her own to make sure that they didn't leave out any key supporter. Her eyes quickly scanned the first page, stopping in alarm when she saw Daphne's name. "Since when did Daphne Wade become a friend of the campaign?" she asked, not bothering to mask her annoyance.

"I know, Jenny. It took me by surprise also, but Michael said to include her. I'm surprised that your father didn't mention it to you."

"My father? What's he got to do with it?"

"Apparently he's been helpful working out things out between Michael and Daphne."

"Working what out?" Jennifer asked, her heart rate quickening.

"Oh, I don't know. It's all so secretive. Just leave it alone, Jennifer. I can tell it's a touchy subject. If Michael wants her there, she comes."

"Just like that? The woman who almost destroyed the campaign? Sent us all into a panic scrambling for weeks to recover and now she's our friend?"

"Jennifer, it's none of our business," Maxine warned.

"Maybe not. But we have a right to question the wisdom of inviting her, don't we?" Jennifer snapped and rushed out of Maxine's office to confront Michael.

Marching into Michael's office unannounced, she

slammed the list on his desk. "Michael, we have to talk." She heard her bitterness spill over into her voice.

Michael's eyes glanced over at the list and he knew immediately the source of the tension. Still, he played it cool. "What's the problem, Jennifer?"

"Why is Daphne Wade coming to your victory party?"

"Because I invited her," he responded in a cool, impersonal tone.

"I see. And since when has she been a supporter?"

"Jennifer, it makes sense if you just try to think logically. She's not the enemy and she is the mother of my son."

Darts jetted out of Jennifer's eyes. "So, there is more to your relationship than you've led me to believe?"

Michael shook his head. "I didn't say that. Sit down. Please."

Sighing, she sat on the edge of the chair on the opposite side of his desk.

"I'm working things out with Daphne legally. And we got a few other things straight, too."

"What things?"

"I was suspicious that Daphne had initiated the hits I took in the press. I asked Moses to find out who leaked the story. His sources came back last week with word that it was Daphne's mother who called the reporter. Apparently she's still bitter over about being deserted by Daphne's biological father and didn't want another man to get away so easily. Daphne was furious that her mother had lied to her.

It threw her into my corner."

Eyes locked, they stared in silence. "Just tell me one thing," she said, trying to remain calm. "Does this mean that you and Daphne are getting back together?"

"Jennifer, don't be silly. I told you that Daphne and I were never a couple."

"Never a couple? That's a laugh! How did you conceive a baby then?"

"You know what I mean. I am not now nor have I ever been in love with her. Am I making myself clear yet?"

"Actually, your story's full of inconsistencies."

"I can't help that. You'll just have to trust me on this, Jennifer."

"Michael, whose brilliant idea was it to invite her to spend election night with us?"

"Your father's. He thought it would look good if we could be there together. It's a political set-up, Jennifer. It's done all the time. I invited her and she accepted. Moses is meeting with Daphne today just to make sure she's okay with how the evening with goes."

"It makes sense that you and my father would conspire on this one. After all, he's as guilty as you are. But I don't have to agree or accept your decision," she said, standing.

"Look, Jennifer, this isn't the time for this discussion. I've got a conference call in ten minutes. I'll come to your office later and we'll talk some more. Okay?"

Rubbing her temples, she tried to soothe the confusion in her head. "Fine," she said, then excused herself and walked dazed back to her office, unsure what to do with the conflicting emotions and sense of loss that crowded her brain and pierced her heart. She glanced around, thankful that the office was empty. Most of the staff were in the field coordinating get-out-the vote activities and making last minute appeals on behalf of their party and candidate. Volunteers were answering phones and contacting churches to remind them of the plan for election day.

Jennifer buried her head in the guest list, comparing it to the names of individuals who'd attended parties on Michael's behalf. She was so focused that she didn't hear anyone approach.

Moses watched his daughter protectively from the open doorway. Her head was bent, her eyes focused on a document, and by the scowl that etched her brow, he assumed that she was engaged in an unpleasant task. "Jenny," he called from a distance.

Startled, Jennifer jumped up. "Dad! What a nice surprise. Come in."

He stepped into her office and hugged her briefly. "We have to talk."

"Okay," she answered quickly. Her eyes searched his for reassurance. "Have a seat. I was just going over these lists for the victory party but it can wait."

"Not here. Get your things." His voice was calm, too calm.

Jennifer studied her father and knew. "It has something to do with my sister, right?" she asked, heart pounding.

"Yes."

"You found her?" Jennifer slumped into her chair, suddenly frightened by the prospect of meeting her sister.

"Get your coat, Jenny. I want to talk away from here."

Alarmed, Jennifer gathered her coat, pocketbook and briefcase without debating her father's wisdom on this. "Okay. But I...I have to stop by and let Maxine know that I'm leaving."

"I've already spoken to Michael. He'll let her know that you had to leave for a while."

She stared wordlessly across the room at her father, her pulse charging. "You've spoken to Michael?" Panic setting in, she stood frozen.

"I'll explain everything, Jennifer. But let's get out of here first."

"Everything, Dad?"

"Everything, I promise."

Foreboding filled her with a sensation of intense sickness and desperation. Unable to speak, she nodded and blindly followed her father out of the office.

A chilling breeze tossed Jennifer's unruly ebony curls across her face. She brushed the hair out of her eyes without losing step with her father. She looked over at him, further pained by what she saw. Moses plowed forward with his hands thrust deep in his pockets, his broad shoulders hunched forward, and his expression desolate. My God, she thought, what could have caused this desperation?

She chewed on her lower lip and stole a look at her father as they neared his car. Bracing for a jolt as big as the one when she'd learned of her half-sister's existence, Jennifer tried to think of the worst possible news. It had to be more than the fact that he'd located his other daughter. What could have caused her father to look so grim? A terrible thought flashed through Jennifer's mind. Suppose he'd finally located her only to find that she was dying or had some rare and particularly deadly tumor? Or maybe, she thought with equal despair, the discovery had destroyed her parents' marriage. It had something to do with her sister. He'd said that.

Her hands trembled as she reached for the door handle. Moses, noticing her shaking hands, captured them in his own for a few seconds.

Jennifer lifted her chin and smiled weakly up at her father. Whatever it was, they would deal with it as a family, she vowed. Feeling crazy with worry, she asked in a small frightened voice. "How did you find her?"

He looked down at his lovely daughter wearily. "Jenny, I'll tell you the whole story. Now get in the car."

"But is she all right?"

"She's fine." He gestured towards the open car door. Moses stepped back to allow Jennifer room to climb in. He shut the solid door and walked to the other side of his black Mercedes Benz.

Puzzled and frightened, Jennifer kept her eyes on her father as he climbed into the driver's seat. "You look sick."

Moses looked over at her. "Jennifer, please. Let's drive over to the beach. Then we can talk in peace."

She nodded, mute with fear. "Does Michael know?"

"I told him that I needed to talk with you. That's all."

Moses left it at that.

Jennifer closed her eyes, imagining all kinds of scenarios, including a loving reunion with her half-sister that seemed unlikely, given the gravity of her father's mood. She shivered, panicked by the possibility that her sister wanted nothing to do with her. Opening her eyes, she decided it was better to keep focused on things that were real, like the route her dad would take to get to the beach.

Moses started up the car. The motor turned over immediately. Its soft hum and her ragged breathing were the only audible sounds. The silence that loomed between them created a physical barrier.

He glanced over at her, his face tight.

Jennifer looked away. Knowing where they were headed, she rested her head against the headrest. He'd tell her in a place where they both felt safe. Sick from the struggle within her, she closed her eyes again, this time to hold back the tears.

Moses kept Jennifer in his peripheral vision. In his mind, he rehearsed a way to tell her how wrong he had been from the beginning. He almost laughed at his arrogance. He had held himself up to Michael as a mentor and father figure worthy of his trust, respect. In the end, he'd disappointed them all.

He had no right to ask for forgiveness and yet he knew that it was necessary, more for the others than for himself. He'd been selfish, stupid, and wrong—very wrong. The remainder of his life he vowed to devote himself to his family—all of them.

Moses pulled into the private road that led to the part of the beach that they both loved. During the summer, the entrance to the beach was manned and only residents with season permits were allowed to enter. When Jennifer was a child, he'd taken her to this beach often. It was their private ritual. Through the years they'd braved the weather and stopped by to embrace the healing derived from the ocean.

Parking the car, Moses looked over at Jennifer and smiled weakly. "Let's go, baby."

Her expression remained clouded with concern as she followed his directions, opened the car door and got out. The ocean breeze whipped through her. She wrapped her arms around her waist, wishing she were clothed in down instead of a waist-length black leather jacket.

Moses popped the trunk and pulled out a blanket he kept for just such occasions. Throwing it over his shoulder, he followed his daughter onto the sand. They each took a corner and together spread the plaid wool blanket—a familiar ritual that they hadn't performed in years. "This reminds me of when you were little," he offered. "Do you remember coming out here with me?"

"You'd call it our private adventure. We'd sneak away

from the house like thieves, stop for bagels and cream cheese, and come here to eat our Sunday morning breakfast before church."

"You always wanted whole grain bagels. Health-conscious, even at seven." They continued filling in the details. "And you would sip hot coffee and I'd drink hot chocolate." She coughed, choked by the warm memories. "You'd start off with, 'What's up with you, baby?'" Tears filled her eyes.

"And you'd whine 'Daddy' in this wondrous small voice, like I'd committed a crime."

She chuckled. "Well, you just expected me to rattle off my week in all its intimate detail and I'd need time to warm up." To her surprise, her voice broke slightly. "That's what this is, isn't it, Dad—a warm-up. So now it's my turn. What's up with you?" she asked as casually as she could manage.

"This is going to be a hard one, Jennifer."

"So let's get on with it. I'm not a seven-year-old filled with illusions, Daddy."

"You're right…I guess I broke all those down when you were twenty," Moses replied, painfully.

"It was time for some reality to hit my life."

"Jennifer, you've grown into the most amazing woman. I'm so proud of you." Moses' gentle gray eyes were teeming with pride and something else.

Jennifer was so filled with emotion that she didn't trust her voice. She hugged her knees to her and nodded for

Moses to continue.

Moses knew that it wasn't fair to stall. "Jennifer, this morning I discovered more about your half-sister."

Her eyes widened. "This morning?"

"Yes. After I called Daphne we agreed to meet. I wanted to talk with her about Michael's victory party. You see, I convinced Michael that she should be there—with the baby. You know, show a united front. Since it was my idea, Michael wanted me to suggest it to Daphne. He wasn't sure how she'd feel about it. Anyway, she agreed to meet me at my office. I arranged it for early in the morning before the staff arrived." Clearing his throat, he continued, "The moment she walked into my office...I...I knew."

Confused, Jennifer studied her father. "Knew what?"

Moses' expression grew grim. "Knew that she was my daughter."

Shock tore through her. Jennifer stared at him. Her mind was unable to comprehend his words. "Excuse me?"

"Daphne is my daughter. I just found out myself. Jennifer, I..."

She held up her hands, begging him to stop. "Daphne is your daughter?" She repeated his words, stunned.

"Yes. I'm afraid so."

"That makes her my half-sister? Daphne...," Jennifer stumbled. "Daphne, the mother of Michael's baby is your daughter! My half-sister...," she repeated in disbelief. "How do you know?"

"Her eyes are smoky gray like yours and mine. Her

hair is thick, curly, and short but she has a striking resemblance to you and to my mother. It took my breath away. So, I asked her about her family. As she talked, I realized that she was describing the woman I'd had an affair with thirty years ago. She got married when Daphne was a toddler and her husband adopted her. Since I'd been adamant that I didn't want a relationship with the baby, her mother didn't bother to notify me."

"Why didn't you say something when Michael first told us about Daphne?" she ranted angrily.

"Daphne uses her stepfather's last name. I didn't recognize her by name. But I took one look at her and knew." Moses shook his head, fighting back the anguish. "Jennifer, I know how shocking this news must be for you. I can't begin to tell you how sorry I am."

"Sorry…" She frowned in disbelief. "For what exactly, Dad? For the affair? For getting Daphne's mother pregnant? Or are you sorry for lying to Mom and me? That she's the mother of Michael's son? What exactly are you sorry for?"

"Jennifer, this was nearly thirty years ago. People weren't as open back then."

"No more excuses, Dad. What you did was wrong!" Bitterness spiked her words.

"I couldn't agree with you more. Jennifer, I made a cowardly decision some twenty-nine years ago and now it has returned to haunt me."

"You mean the decision not to be a part of your daughter's life?"

"Jennifer, it's not your pity I want. It's your willingness to work this through with your mother and me."

"This is insane!" Jennifer leaped up, wanting to run. Needing to run.

Moses jumped up, grabbing Jennifer's arm. "Not this time, Jennifer!" he said in a harsh, raw voice. "We're going to deal with this together."

Jennifer scrambled to find words to describe the way she felt. She'd initiated the search but hadn't anticipated this horrible twist of fate. Hadn't expected to discover that she and her sister shared more than paternal genes. "It's your mess! So why do we have to deal at all?"

"Because we're family! Damn it."

"Mom." Her voice dropped an octave as she sank back down on the blanket. "You told her?"

"Of course."

"And…?"

"She was as shocked as you are."

Jennifer groaned. "This is just too much, Dad. Daphne is my half-sister." Shaking her head, she collapsed on her knees and rocked back and forth. "Did you tell her?"

"Yes."

"Dad, stop making me pull this out of you!" She shot him a cold look.

"Yes, I told Daphne. We talked for a couple of hours. She's a bright, level-headed young woman who grew up without illusions—thanks to my cruelty."

"Lovely," Jennifer replied sarcastically. She wavered, trying to comprehend what she was learning. "And Michael?"

"I'll tell him after the elections are over."

"More secrets. Haven't you learned?"

"It's safer to keep this secret two more days."

"Won't Daphne tell him?"

"No, we agreed that it would be a mistake."

Sobered by the notion, tears blinded her pearl gray eyes, giving them the appearance of smoke. She looked away from her father's anguished face, not wanting it to sway her tortured emotions. She rammed her fist into her cupped hand. Swallowing the sob in her throat, she looked up. "What now?"

"It's up to you. Would you like to meet her?"

No, she wasn't interested in meeting the woman who had a baby by the man she loved. "No, Dad," she said with a finality that matched the depth of the despair that had settled deep inside. "Let's go. I have work to do."

Jennifer rose slowly, her eyes focused on the waves that tumbled furiously against the shoreline, signaling that a storm was near. And a storm raged in her heart as well. She took slow, deep breaths trying to still the internal thunder. She lingered on the beach a few minutes, drinking in the sounds of seagulls and water meeting land. Was this what her mother meant by patience? Could she possibly remain steady in face of this crisis? she asked herself.

Moses eased over to his daughter, longing to take her

in his arms and soothe her as he had when she was a child. "Jennifer, sure you don't want to meet her?"

She turned in her father's direction, face devoid of emotion. "Don't push this, Dad," she warned. "I'm going to finish my work on the campaign, then head back to L.A. That's where I belong right now."

"Head back to L.A.?"

"Yes, right after the elections. And, Dad, I forbid you to discuss my business with Michael. I don't want him distracted at this point."

"I have no intention of talking with Michael until after the election. But, Jennifer, you can't run away this time. We need to deal with this as a family. Isn't that why you came home?"

Her eyes narrowed. It was incredulous, unfair, and conclusive. "I'm not running away. I will finish my work. I'll meet my sister…someday. I'm just not ready for that yet."

Moses studied his daughter. "And Michael? I thought that you cared about him?"

She looked away. "Yes. But it doesn't matter. This complicates our lives so completely that there's no hope for a future with Michael." She stopped, choking back a sob.

"I'm sorry you feel that way. Michael's not in love with Daphne and I don't think that she's in love with him either. They just need time to work out arrangements for the baby."

"My nephew, you mean," she said, softly.

"And my grandson."

Their eyes locked in guarded acceptance of the tangled web. "We all need time," Moses concluded. "By the way, Daphne's decided not to come to the election night party."

"That's good."

"Will you be all right?"

"In time." Jennifer wrapped her arms around her waist. "What about Mom?"

"Like you…this will take some time," he admitted sadly. "Ready to go?"

"Very." She bent to gather the blanket in her arms. "Dad, promise me you won't tell Michael until after I've left?"

Moses nodded, thinking it wrong for her to leave now but it wasn't his call. "I promise, baby."

"One more thing, Dad."

"Yes."

"Max."

"What about him?"

"Did you meet him?"

"Yes. He's beautiful," Moses said proudly.

"So Michael says. Send me a picture of him, would you?"

"Yes."

Thirteen

The polls closed. Michael Wingate was declared the winner in over half of the precincts. The remainder pointed towards victory. Laughter and music floated through the ballroom as the election night party began to gather momentum.

Jennifer twisted a finger around the gold chain that adorned her neckline as she greeted supporters. She wore a white cashmere, cable-knit ribbed turtleneck, and straight skirt with a side slit. She held her head high, giving the impression of grace, poise and confidence. No one would have guessed that the past forty-eight hours had left her numb, indifferent to the celebratory atmosphere that surrounded her.

Jennifer was determined to keep the tangled mess at an emotional distance until she could take the time to process what she'd learned. She was also certain that she needed time and distance in order to make that happen. She further rationalized her decision to leave by saying that once Michael found out that she and Daphne were sisters, he would need time to sort out his feelings as well. She wished that she could say goodbye to him but knew that wasn't possible. Instead, she would have to face Michael without showing him the fear, hurt and confusion that she assumed lay naked in her eyes.

Jennifer had it all planned. She'd stop by the suite and wish him well, make her excuses, then ease out while Michael was focused on making his victory speech. By the time he took the stage, she'd be at Kennedy preparing to board the night flight to L.A. Only Moses and Sarah knew of her plans.

Checking her watch, Jennifer realized that she had only an hour before the car would pick her up and take her to Kennedy. She headed to his suite, greeted the staffers who were covering the door, and walked into a crowded living room. People were focused on the TV, watching the constant updates on national and local campaigns. Michael Wingate was leading with a twenty percent margin but since only half the precincts were accounted for, the anchors held off on declaring victory. Still, since Michael's victory was within reach, the mood was cautiously optimistic.

Jennifer studied Michael without his knowing she'd entered the room. His attention seemed equally divided between the television reports and his guests. He was even more arresting in face of certain victory than he was after they'd made love. She longed to go to him but stood frozen in the same spot.

"You did it, Michael!' she wanted to shout, but restrained the impulse. For her the moment was clouded by sadness because she knew that she wouldn't be there when he was declared a winner. Hoping to preserve the night, she memorized each powerful gesture, facial expression, and the sound of his voice.

Michael looked up and met Jennifer's intense gaze. He stopped talking mid-sentence as an easy smile crept over his lips and he crossed to her.

Does he know? she wondered. She lowered her thick, dark lashes, fighting to maintain her composure.

"Jennifer, I've been waiting for you." His voice was low and seductive.

She lifted her chin and looked at him. "Michael, I'm so proud of you."

He gathered her face in his massive hands. His thumbs gently stroked her temples as his mahogany eyes drank hers in. "We did it." He kissed her gently before all that were gathered. Pulling away, he whispered, "I've missed you. Come to me later, please."

Eyes tearing, knees weak, heart splitting in two, she lied. "Yes."

He leaned to kiss the tip of her nose before pressing his lips to hers again. He lingered this time, deepening his kiss slightly.

Succumbing to the forceful magnetism of his slow,

thoughtful kiss, Jennifer leaned into his hard steady body for support.

Michael pulled away at the first sound of clapping. "Later," he whispered, eyes soaking her up again. He turned away from Jennifer and acknowledged the applause for the kiss with a broad smile and easy laugh.

She was mute and flushed with a combination of desire and embarrassment. Her misty eyes quickly scanned the room. Finding their target, she caught the pained look in her father's eyes. He stood with the rest but his hands did not applaud. Instead, they rested on his hips. He smiled weakly in his daughter's direction.

Michael grabbed Jennifer's hand and together they walked into the middle of the group.

Moses stepped forward, handing Michael and Jennifer each a glass of Moet champagne.

Michael held his flute of bubbly up towards her.

"Before we head down to greet the others, I would like you to join me in a private toast." Michael's eyes scanned the room, then bore into Jennifer's.

Reaching for their glasses, the others spoke aloud in agreement. There was much to celebrate.

"To you, Jennifer Mariah Kelly, I offer a special thank you for coming into my world at this critical junction in my life. I could not have won without you by my side, especially the last four weeks."

Biting her quivering lip, Jennifer tipped her glass to Michael and spoke softly. "And to you, our amazing candidate and senator-elect, I pray for your continued strength, success and happiness."

He kissed her gently. Turning to the others, Michael continued with the toasting. "Each of you has added immensely to my life. I thank you from the depth of my soul for your support, love and enduring encouragement." Glasses clicked. Familiar voices chimed in words of support and appreciation as Michael Logan Wingate prepared to move from being a candidate to being a member of the U.S. Senate.

Jennifer was immune to the excitement around her. Her thoughts were arrested on Michael's tender pledge to her. Feeling like an imposter, she wished the night could end differently. For a moment, she wavered, considered, and then rejected staying on for one last night of passion. Bravely, she whispered into Michael's ear, "Darling, I have to leave you now."

Alarmed, he turned to her. "Where are you going?"

Forcing a reassuring smile, she replied, "To make sure everything is set for your grand entry."

"I want to walk in with you by my side."

"Walk in with your mother and sister," she urged. "That's the picture that we want to capture."

"Okay, my wise one. I'll grant you this final wish, but from now on…"

She held up her hand, silencing Michael. "Yes. From now on…," Jennifer said, before signaling to her father.

"Dad, will you and Mom please walk with me downstairs," she asked, her eyes pleading.

Clearing his throat, Moses agreed.

Jennifer slipped her hand into Michael's, squeezing it gently. He pulled her hand to his lips. "Leave when you see me exit the ballroom. I'll meet you up here," he whispered seductively.

She hoped her face didn't reflect the sadness she felt. Forcing cheer, she kissed him softly on his cheek then rushed out of the suite before she changed her mind.

The next few minutes were a blur. She slipped her father a letter for Michael, retrieved her luggage from the storage room and said a teary good-bye to her parents, promising to call when she arrived in L.A. She paused, turned to her father, and reminded him to send her a picture of Max. Without waiting for his reply, she got into the limo and was rapidly consumed by a deep sense of loss.

Alone with her thoughts, Jennifer rested her head against the leather seat and asked herself if she'd made the right decision. Just as quickly, she banished the thought, knowing that she'd had no choice. It was her father's responsibility to tell Michael that Daphne was his daughter. Michael would need time to resolve the hurt that would accompany such a painful disclosure. After that, they'd have to see what would happen next. Although several scenarios came to mind, she felt no need to second-guess Michael's response to the news. Soon enough she'd know.

As the limo entered the Merritt Parkway heading

towards Kennedy Airport, Jennifer tried to imagine where Michael would be right now. Probably circling the ballroom, shaking hands, thanking his supporters, and looking for her. A shiver raced through her body as she recalled his invitation for her to join him after the party. Closing her eyes against tears, she prayed that Michael would understand.

Jennifer pulled her coat snugly around her. She was certain that she was in love with him and she now knew that he was in love with her. What she didn't know was if their love for each other was strong enough to overcome the obstacles that lay in their path.

A smiling Michael Wingate stepped up to the podium and waited until the enthusiastic crowd quieted. "My friends, we've reached this pivotal moment humbled by the fullness of the experience. As I look around, I see the faces of those who stood by me throughout this challenging race. To those voters I did not have the opportunity to physically meet, I thank you for trusting me to serve you in the U.S. Senate."

Michael paused for the spontaneous cheers, applause, and shouts of support, then continued. "By your vote of confidence, it's clear that we've had a meeting of the minds and hearts. I thank you for your support and promise not to disappoint you." The room erupted again. As the crowd settled down, he turned to face his mother and sister and his eyes filled with tears. He introduced his family, thanking them for their love and support. Amid resounding applause, he added, "My soul drinks from the sweet waters of forgiveness. I feel truly blessed to have been nurtured, encouraged and supported by you from the start." Michael went on to thank Moses for his leadership and his staff for their enduring support and dedication, reminding them that the work had just begun.

The entire time Michael was speaking, his eyes searched the audience for Jennifer. He couldn't understand why she wasn't either right up front or on the stage with the others. Something must have happened.

❧❦❧

"Going back to L.A.!" Michael spat out the words angrily.

"Yes. She should be at Kennedy by now." Moses purposely kept his voice low, not wanting to draw attention to their discussion.

There were about twenty-five people in the living room. Moses and Michael were cloistered in one of the bedrooms.

"You mean Jennifer knew when she came up to the suite that she was leaving?" Michael asked. Moses nodded. Then Michael looked up at Moses and narrowed his eyes.

"You knew she was leaving, didn't you?"

"Yes, I knew, Michael."

"Why didn't you tell me before now when I could have done something about it?"

"Because I promised my daughter to hold off until after the victory party. She didn't want anything to spoil your night."

"But why, Moses?" He stared at his mentor and friend.

"Why would she just take off without talking to me? What's going on? None of this is making sense. Was it because I invited Daphne? You explained all that to her, didn't you?" Michael sank his hands into his pockets, confused.

Moses knew that he couldn't postpone the inevitable any longer. Michael deserved an explanation. "Michael, sit down, please. We have to talk."

Eyeing Moses suspiciously, Michael slumped into the nearest armchair. His fisted hands reflected the raging tension that fired his body.

In the tense silence Moses gazed into a pair of confused, dark eyes. "You once asked me why I never ran for a political office myself. I think I gave you some vague answer to your question, along the lines that it requires too much personal sacrifice. As you now know, that was only part of my reason. In truth, my personal life couldn't stand up to the scrutiny."

"What does Jennifer's leaving have to do with your personal life?"

"Everything," Moses replied.

Michael felt an inkling of understanding about the conversation's direction. "You found your other daughter, didn't you?"

"I did."

"Then Jennifer's leaving is even more confusing because she told me that she came home to find her sister. Why would she leave just when that has happened?"

Moses cleared his throat. "Because there's more to the story." He began slowly, allowing the story to unfold gradually. Repeating the story again helped Moses understand his feelings as well.

Michael's heart raced wildly as a shudder passed through him. The absurdity of the coincidence was beyond his comprehension. Too stunned to speak, he just glared at Moses. "Sarah and, my God, Jennifer... They know, don't they?" It explained so many things, especially Jennifer's sudden departure. "When did you tell Jennifer?"

"Two days ago. The same day I found out. Remember when I called your office and told you that I needed to talk with Jennifer?" Michael nodded. "Well, that's when I told her."

"She didn't say anything to me," Michael mumbled, stunned.

"No, she didn't, purposely. Jennifer's strong like her mother. She didn't want you to worry or get upset at such a critical juncture in your candidacy."

"What about Sarah?" Michael asked, still too shocked to know how he felt about the news.

"I'm married to a truly remarkable woman, and we've raised a confident and compassionate daughter. I say that without diminishing the pain they're both in." Moses' voice sounded strained.

Michael saw anguish in his friend's eyes. His own throat felt clogged with emotion. He coughed, clearing it.

"Tell me more about how Jennifer reacted."

"I took her to our favorite beach. It was deserted. We wrapped up in a blanket and talked for a long time." He smiled weakly. "She was upset naturally and pushed away my attempts to comfort her. I asked her if she wanted to meet Daphne but she said she wasn't ready for that yet. She also said that she needed some space and thought you would too. That's when she told me that she was going back to L.A. election night." Tears welled again. "I wanted to try and talk her out of it. Wanted to tell her that it was time to stop running but I had no right to take that position. So, I agreed to keep her secret from you and to even help her make a clean exit." He shook his head sadly. "But before she left, she asked me to send her a picture of Max." He paused, collecting his emotions. "I was encouraged by that. At least she's not rejecting the baby. Still, it's gonna take time for her to come around. We owe her that much respect."

"And she left while I was giving my acceptance speech because she didn't want me to try to influence her decision?"

"Yes. I guess that's part of it..." Moses hesitated,

knowing he was about to reveal more about his daughter's feelings than he might have a right to. What the hell, he thought. We've been living with secrecy far too long. "She wants to give you both time to process the new entanglements in your lives. That's all I can say..." Purposely vague, Moses stopped there.

Michael frowned. "I hear you, Moses, and I appreciate the position I'm putting you in, but it's still not adding up. Didn't she say anything else?"

"Oh, she gave her mother and me all kinds of reasons for why she had to leave without talking with you, but I think she couldn't face you, Michael." Moses paused to carefully consider his next words. He knew that Jennifer was in love with Michael, but he didn't know whether Michael was committed to her. As her father and Michael's political advisor, he felt awkward. He also didn't dare do anything that Jennifer might construe as betrayal. So, he danced a bit, hoping Michael would understand. "We kind of swept Jennifer up in the middle of her life and asked her to give us a few months. Given all that has happened, she felt it was time for her to return immediately to the West Coast—for a while, anyway. I didn't get the feeling that it would be forever. She has several good reasons to want to come back home. Knowing my daughter, it will be on her terms, though."

Trying to understand, Michael pressed, "Any idea what those terms would be?"

Moses shrugged. "Not sure. But I think it might have

something to do with you."

Michael shook his head. "It's kind of hard to do anything with 3,000 miles separating us," he mumbled, then stood and began to walk aimlessly around the room. This explained the pained, distant look in Jennifer's eyes. He only wished that she'd trusted him enough to come to him. He shook his head. "I just can't believe that this is happening. Wait a minute." He turned to Moses with a perplexed expression. "You met the mother of my son and instantly knew that she was your daughter?"

"No, it wasn't exactly like that. Of course there was a physical familiarity. You must have seen the likeness, too?"

"The first time I saw Jennifer I felt like I'd met her before. I even commented on it. But since I wasn't even thinking along those lines I didn't make the connection. Those arresting gray eyes..." Michael sank back into the chair. "Moses, how did you know for sure?"

"Before I told her of my suspicions, I got her to talking about her parents, which led to a discussion about her biological father. I asked her what her mother's maiden name was and then I knew for certain." He paused, remembering their conversation.

Michael prodded Moses cautiously. "So, you told Daphne that she was your daughter?"

"Yes. At first I was hesitant, but then I decided there had been enough lies. She was more stunned than angry."

Moses paused, remembering that moment so well. "It was incredible actually. We both cried and hugged." His eyes misted. "Daphne seems to have had a good relationship with her stepfather. Do you know him?"

"Not well, but I know he's been a good father to Daphne."

Moses smiled at Michael. "Yes...anyway, I went back to her house with her and met my grandson. He's a beautiful, happy baby."

"Yes, I'm sure you did. How's Sarah taking all this?"

"Sarah's hurt and worried about Jennifer. She wanted to go to L.A. with her but Jennifer wouldn't have it."

Overcome with the implications of all that had transpired in the last two days, Michael stared at his friend and mentor, wondering what to do next. He sighed. "What do you intend on doing now, Moses?"

"Slow down a bit. Concentrate on my marriage. Get to know my other daughter. Give Sarah a chance to get comfortable with Daphne and Max." He paused. "Sarah's always wanted to travel. I plan to take her to Europe and Africa for six weeks or so next summer...just the two of us."

"Sounds good. Any concerns about being away for that long?"

"Some, but I'll get over them. It's time I gave more to the people I love. Besides, I've got people I can trust to run things while I'm away. Another lesson that I hope to pass on to you is not to wait until you're sixty-seven to make your family a priority."

"I hear you," Michael agreed thoughtfully. "You've

been wonderful to me and for me, Moses. Now we have another bond through Max."

"Just how will you work things out?"

"Excuse me?"

"What are your plans?"

Michael smiled. "I'm sure you're not talking about my career." A great deal had happened in the last few days, but Michael was beginning to feel in control of his life again. He knew exactly how he wanted it to go. "I was never in love with Daphne."

"I understand that."

Michael exchanged a firm look with Moses and shared with him his plans as far as Daphne and Max were concerned. He paused. "As for Jennifer…well, we'll just have to see…," Michael said, studying Moses. "I guess in the long run we're judged by how we handle our responsibilities, huh?"

"Got that right, son, and you more than most. You'll be in the midst of public scrutiny from here on out. Can you deal with it?"

"I can deal, Moses. It's odd. I've worked so hard to keep my record clean and now…but, there's no need to go down that road again. Trust me, I'll take care of my end of things."

"I'm sorry that we had to talk tonight on the one night when you should be celebrating."

"The celebration is over. The hard work begins now."

"That's a good attitude."

Moses took this moment to excuse himself. Yawning, he stood to leave. "Well, it's been one hell of a day, Senator."

Michael chuckled, liking the sound of that title. "I agree."

Walking towards the door, Moses added, "Take a few moments alone. I'll cover for you. Oh..." Moses paused, reaching deep into the pocket of his slacks to pull out a letter. "Jennifer left this for you." He extended the slightly tattered envelope in Michael's direction. "Come by the house in the morning," Moses added before walking out.

Michael looked at the envelope and slumped onto the edge of the bed to tear it open.

Michael,

Please forgive me for leaving without a word. But by now you will have spoken with my father and maybe even understand my decision to leave so suddenly.

Michael, I feel sorry that it was necessary to hit you with such shocking news on your night of triumph. But, as you can imagine, the celebratory spirit got tangled with the harshness of reality.

I've asked myself repeatedly if I'm running again. Though I haven't quite answered that question satisfactorily, I feel that time and distance are essential.

Be assured that I'm in shock but not angry, so I guess that in itself qualifies this goodbye as different from the last one. There's something else that makes this time different, and that's the deep loss I already feel from leaving you. But I'm sure you will agree, my love, that the fact that Daphne is my sister changes everything. And Max...my God...your son is my nephew... Time and distance. I need both to sort things out.

I must say goodbye now...not for long, though. I'm certain that our paths will cross again soon. Until then, please take good care of my nephew and yourself.

Forever,

Jennifer

Michael dropped the letter to his side and lay back against the pillows. She was right, he thought, their lives had taken a complete turn. Time and distance... He considered her emotional request and smiled. Closing his eyes, Michael knew that the storm had passed, leaving in its wake the cleanup and rebuilding. Suddenly anxious for the celebration to officially end, he strolled into the living room to say goodnight to his guests.

Fourteen

Michael was lost in his thoughts as the American Airline jet touched down at LAX. It had been five weeks and six days since he'd heard Jennifer's voice, held her in his arms or told her that he loved her.

He hadn't called her because she'd asked him for time. Instead of violating that condition, he'd eagerly listened for clues as to how Jennifer was doing from Moses and Sarah. Since he was still on shaky ground with Sarah, she didn't offer him much insight about her daughter's mental state. All he really knew was that she hadn't accepted another job yet. But before he left, he'd made a point of telling both Sarah and Moses he was headed to L.A. to see Jennifer.

Michael peeked out of the window as the plane approached its gate. He'd sent Jennifer an e-mail before he left but she hadn't responded. As the plane slowly taxied into position, he came up with an alternative plan just in case she wasn't at the gate to meet him.

As the jet engines halted, he unhooked his seat belt and bolted out of his seat. Michael retrieved his bag from the overhead, filed out of the plane and hustled up the jetway. As he emerged, his eyes anxiously scanned the waiting room.

🎋🦋🎋

Jennifer's heartbeat quickened. Her lips curved into a broad smile. There he is, she thought. "Michael," she called out as she crossed the room to meet him.

Michael spun around just as Jennifer reached his side. He dropped his suitcase and swept her into his arms. "Jennifer," he whispered, bending to kiss her moist, welcoming lips.

Reluctantly, he released his grip and looked down into her smoky, velvet eyes as if he couldn't believe that she'd come.

"I'm here, Michael," she said softly.

"Yes, you are," he replied, smiling.

"Did you have any doubt that I'd come?" she asked, her eyes blurred with tears of joy.

"Actually, I did," he admitted.

"You could have just called, you know."

"E-mail was safer. You did get it?"

Jennifer laughed. "Yes and it read like a telegram. 'Arriving on American Airlines, Flight 224, at 12:40.' Stop.

'Please come.' Stop. Not the most romantic invitation, but I got the point," she teased.

Michael traced Jennifer's full lips with his finger. "I was saving the romance until I got here. Besides, I couldn't take the chance that you'd tell me not to come." He replaced his fingers with his lips. They touched gently, holding back the hunger.

"How'd you know that I'd check my e-mail in time?"

"I didn't. So I mentioned it to Sarah, knowing that she'd call you."

"Pretty clever, Senator."

"You're telling me." He bent to meet her kiss more thoroughly this time. Pulling away, he said, "Let's get out of here. I'm starving."

"I know just the place to satisfy your hunger."

"Really," Michael replied, eyebrows arched playfully.

"Let's start with the kind of hunger that can be satisfied by food. I packed a picnic lunch and thought we'd take a ride along the coast and stop when we find a deserted beach."

"Sounds like a plan," Michael said, picking up his bag with his left hand and locking the fingers of his right hand with Jennifer's free hand.

As they walked towards the exit, Michael talked all the way. He filled Jennifer in on the post-campaign happenings. Maxine was in D.C. looking for an apartment for herself. Jerry had accepted a position with the Democratic National Committee. He'd hired a chief-of-staff who was in the process of interviewing candidates for full time staff positions. And no, he hadn't begun to search for a place to live in D.C.

Jennifer listened intently. Michael seemed to be moving on with his life without her, but she hadn't given him much choice. By the time they reached her car, her euphoria had passed.

Michael caught the stab of pain in her eyes. "What's wrong?" he asked.

She frowned. "I was just wishing that I could have been there," she said, then refocused her attention on finding her keys and unlocking the trunk.

Michael grabbed her hand and pulled her to him. "You made the right decision, you know. We needed time. We're together now. And if I have my way, we'll never be separated again," Michael said, regretting his words as soon as they left his mouth. He'd promised himself that he would not press Jennifer.

Michael looked into Jennifer's eyes and knew instantly that he'd erred by sharing his feelings with her before they'd had a chance to talk out the things that had forced them apart in the first place. He started to say something else to lighten the moment, but she walked away before he had a chance. He cursed softly.

Jennifer opened her car door and slipped in behind the steering wheel, feeling instantly comforted by the structure the tight space provided. Her heart pounded wildly as she fought the mounting anxiety. She'd dreamed of this moment, prayed that Michael would come for her soon, and now that he was here, she was confused and afraid.

Once Michael was settled in the seat beside her, Jennifer started the car, exiting the airport parking lot. She drove in silence, trying to figure out the best way to discuss her concerns. She remembered the range of emotions that she'd experienced. It had rained for eight days straight when she first returned. The daily thunderstorms had resulted in severe mudslides along the coastal highways, preventing her from traveling north along the ocean. The confinement had given her plenty of time to think.

By the time the clouds blew out to sea, Jennifer had decided that she wanted to meet her sister and nephew. She was equally clear that her love for Michael was strengthened, not diminished by the crisis. But she still had many unanswered questions. For one, she wanted to know if Daphne had agreed to the joint custody arrangement for Max or was holding out for more.

Jennifer glanced nervously over at Michael. There were so many things she wanted to say to him, but she had no idea where to begin. She released one hand from the steering wheel and laced her fingers with Michael's. A smile formed on her lips as he raised her hand to his lips and kissed it.

"You better either stay focused on the road or skip the picnic and let me make love to you instead," he said.

"Not just yet, Senator," Jennifer said, resting her hand on his thigh. She stroked it lovingly while her thoughts drifted to the last time they'd made love.

"Maybe I should drive," Michael said hoarsely.

Jennifer chuckled. "I'll behave," she said, pulling her hand away and placing it back on the steering wheel. "I've missed you...that's all."

Michael leaned over and kissed Jennifer's cheek. "Not nearly as much as I've missed you," he said softly.

Jennifer signaled her exit off the freeway and turned north onto Pacific Coast Highway.

The ocean lay naked in front of them. It was a route she knew well, yet it felt as if she were seeing its expansive beauty for the first time. Michael made the difference. His presence heightened all her senses.

"Have you driven up the coast before?" she asked.

"No. I've come to L.A. many times but I never took the time to explore beyond the city limits." His eyes took in the homes perched along the cliffs and the sea battering the shoreline. Michael felt as if he'd entered a different world. "I can see why you like to come here."

Stealing another glance at the ocean, Jennifer nodded.

"The Pacific Ocean has a different kind of intensity and beauty than the Atlantic has."

"Your apartment's in a beach community, isn't it?" he asked, trying to remember the details from one of their previous conversations.

"Yes. I live a little south of here in the town of Santa Monica. It has a boardwalk, bike trails and walking beaches, but it's also less private than the Malibu area where we're headed.

"But you chose to live in Santa Monica."

Jennifer nodded. "It's closer to downtown L.A. and very near UCLA. When I want to be alone, I head north, though."

Michael rubbed his hand along Jennifer's thigh. She was wearing worn jeans that clung to her long, shapely legs.

He removed his hand before it wandered to a more intimate place.

"What have you been doing since you got back, Jenny?" he asked.

Jennifer shot Michael a look of concern. He'd just given her the opening she needed. "Not much, really. I've spent most of the time reading and thinking," she said, her voice trailing off as she tried to think of the right words to describe how she was feeling.

"Did you come to any conclusions?" he asked.

"Some."

"Care to share them with me?"

"I want to have a relationship with my sister and nephew," she said without mentioning what she wanted from him.

"That's good," he said, then hesitated, wondering if it was a good time to tell her how he'd worked things out with Daphne. "I've done a lot of thinking too," he started. "And I've made some progress. The most important step was getting down on paper what my relationship and responsibility to my son will be. It went smoother than I'd imagined. Two days ago Daphne and I signed a joint custody agreement. I'm going to buy a house and hire a nanny so that Max can live with me when I'm in Connecticut."

Jennifer's shoulder slumped as she released a sigh of relief. He'd answered one of her questions without being asked. "I'm sure that you're relieved," she said.

"Very. I'm going to sell the townhouse and buy a single family house with a yard for him to play in," he continued.

"Makes sense," she replied.

"You're awfully quiet about this. Should we talk about something else?"

"I'm fine. Tell me more, Michael," she pressed, hoping that in the process he'd tell her why he'd come.

"I'm getting better at caring for Max by myself," he said, then chuckled. "My first afternoon alone with him was a bit scary. Daphne's in the process of weaning him off breast milk. When I offered Max a bottle, he threw it on the floor and screamed for twenty minutes straight. I panicked and called my mother. You can't imagine how happy I was when she arrived and Max settled down. I guess he's just used to a woman's touch."

Jennifer reached over and grasped Michael's hand. "It takes time."

"Yeah. I guess."

"Mom told me that you brought Max over to the house."

"I did. Are you okay with that?"

"Max is their grandchild and you're like a son to them, Michael," she said without looking at him.

Michael nodded. "That's true. Sarah was terrific with Max. Moses seemed nervous."

Jennifer smiled, remembering the stories her mom had told her about when she was a baby. "Dad's never been comfortable around babies. He likes them when they can talk back and go to the potty independently."

"So I gathered. Anyway, it was wonderful to watch Max interact with Sarah. She and I are in a rebuilding stage. I think bringing Max over to see her settled some of her concerns. She now knows that I intend on being an active parent."

Jennifer gripped the steering wheel as she steadied her emotion. "I...I just wish that I could have been there," she said softly.

"You will be the next time," Michael reassured her.

She cleared her throat, then plunged forward with the question that was really on her mind. "When are you bringing Daphne over?"

Michael studied Jennifer. "I want you to meet Daphne first." He watched as her fingers tensed around the steering wheel. They had to get past this point. "Finding your sister was your idea, Jennifer. I know that it was a shock to find out that Daphne was the missing link, but I hope you still want to bring your family together."

Jennifer's expression grew serious. "Have you broached the idea with Daphne?"

"Yes. We've talked about it at length, actually. Daphne's looking forward to meeting you, Jennifer."

Jennifer took a few seconds before responding. "What did you tell her?"

"That I'm in love with you."

"And she still wants to meet me?"

"Yes."

"Why?" Jennifer asked, not sure if she'd feel the same way if the situation had been reversed.

"For several reasons. Daphne appreciates the fact that you initiated the search to find her. She admires your courage and generosity. But more importantly, she's not in love with me, Jennifer."

"Oh…but the photo in the paper…the kiss."

"It was computer-doctored, Jennifer." He looked hesitantly at her. "Does it bother you to talk about Daphne?" he asked.

She turned to meet his questioning glance. "No. It's okay. I want to talk about her, Michael. After all, she is my sister," she said, her voice controlled.

Michael released a sigh. "I've been so scared of losing you," he said quietly.

She reached for his hand. "That's not possible, Michael. I'm in love with you."

He squeezed her fingers. "I'm in love with you too, Jennifer."

Tears formed in Jennifer's eyes, clouding her vision. She blinked, clearing her eyes again. "If I come home, could you arrange for me to meet Daphne and Max?"

Michael nodded, too moved to speak. "You're incredible, Jennifer," he finally got out. "I'd be happy to arrange a meeting. Are you coming home?"

"Yes, I think so," she responded. "What I mean is that I bought my ticket, but I still haven't told Mom anything definite." She looked over at Michael. "Do you think next week is too soon?"

Michael wished that they weren't driving so that he could take Jennifer into his arms. He settled for brushing the back of his hand along her cheek. "It's not soon enough for me. I want you home for good."

Jennifer smiled. "Yes," she whispered. That's what she wanted as well. Clearing her throat, she asked, "What will you do for the holidays?"

"I'll probably spend Christmas with my mother and sister."

Jennifer glanced at Michael. "I wish we could spend New Year's together," she said.

"Me too," he replied.

"You could come after Christmas," she suggested, remembering her mother's proposal that they blend their families for the holidays.

"Or you could come to Connecticut and stay through New Year's," he said.

"I know." She hesitated, hating her cowardice. "Actually Mom had another idea. She was wondering if we could all have Christmas dinner together this year."

"Our families?" Michael asked, needing clarification.

"Yes. You, your mother, sister, I suppose," she said tentatively, knowing that her mother had also talked about inviting Daphne and Max. Funny, she'd always dreamed of a big family dinner for the holidays. One where they'd need to bring in extra chairs for the dining-room table and maybe even set up a kid's table alongside the adult one. But she had never considered such a complicated formula.

"That's an interesting idea. I'd have to discuss it with my mother. Holidays have been really tough since my dad died. We haven't felt like celebrating," he said.

"Maybe now that you have Max you'll feel more like celebrating," she offered.

"Maybe," he replied thoughtfully.

Jennifer peeked over at Michael, wanting to tell him that Sarah was open to inviting Daphne and Max to dinner as well. But was she herself?

"It would be low key. Just the six of us," she said, deciding not to reveal her cards just yet.

"Mom might like that. I'll ask her," he repeated, pleased that they might be together for Christmas. The thought cheered him and he hoped that his mother would agree.

Jennifer flipped on her turn signal and swerved the car into the turn lane. There weren't any cars in the parking lot, she noted. "It looks like we'll have the beach all to ourselves."

As the oncoming traffic stopped at the red light, she

turned into the parking lot and drove into the nearest vacant space. "Thank God we're here 'cause I'm not sure if I could have driven another mile," she said. Turning off the engine, she thought about her sister. How would it feel to look into the eyes of another person and see herself? Would she be jealous of her father's firstborn and the mother of her lover's baby? Could she really pull this off and welcome Daphne and Max into her life? Hands clammy, heart slamming against her ribs, she reached into the backseat and grabbed her sweatshirt. "I need to get out of here. Do you mind grabbing the picnic basket and blanket from the trunk?" she asked as she dashed from the car, suddenly desperate for air.

Baffled by the sudden shift in Jennifer's mood, Michael started to follow her. Instead, he stood still for a moment, watching her back as she descended the hill to the sand. Then he quickly changed into his boots, grabbed the picnic basket and blanket, and raced off down the beach after her. He wasn't willing to let her go this time.

Jennifer was walking slowly. Head bowed, hands thrust in the pockets of her hooded sweatshirt. A cool breeze slapped a film of salt water against her cheeks. Her eyes stung.

Michael grabbed her arm and halted her retreat.

Jennifer whipped around to face him. Her face was stained with tears.

"What's the matter?" he asked, his own heart aching as he drank in the sadness that he read in her eyes.

"Mom suggested that we invite Daphne and Max to dinner too," she blurted out as her body collapsed. She sobbed openly.

Michael dropped the blanket and basket and gathered Jennifer into his arms, covering her face with kisses. "We could, you know."

"Do you think she'd come?"

"She might."

"Oh Michael, I'm so scared," she sobbed.

Tears filled his eyes. He blinked them back. And then, as if he couldn't control himself, he whispered, "I want to marry you, Jennifer."

Stunned by the suddenness of his proposal, Jennifer froze. Her hands dropped to her sides as she stared at Michael, speechless. "How can we talk about marriage when our lives are in complete chaos?"

Michael gathered Jennifer's face in his hands. "Because I can't live without you. Yes, we still have major hurdles in front of us, but if we're a team nothing will stop us," he whispered, holding her face close to his.

Jennifer choked back a sob. "Oh, Michael…I do love you. And I want to love your son." She lifted onto her toes and welcomed his slow, gentle kiss.

"Then tell me that you'll never leave me again," he pleaded when the kiss ended. He needed the reassurance.

"I'll never leave you, Michael," she promised.

Michael lifted Jennifer three feet into the air and swung her around. "You'll marry me then?"

She laughed. "I'll marry you, Michael, but could we keep our plans between us until our lives are more settled?"

"Jennifer, we have to promise each other that there'll be no more secrets," he implored, "not even happy ones."

"You're right, Michael. No more secrets."

"Besides, I think our families need some good news." "Are you absolutely sure you want to marry me, Michael?" Michael drew Jennifer into his arms and gently eased her onto the blanket.

She lay back, her eyes searching his for answers.

Resting on one elbow, Michael traced his fingertips across her lips. "I've never felt so sure of anything in my life," he said, lowering his body to meet hers.

Their lips barely touched, Jennifer whispered, "Yes, oh Michael, yes." She reached up and locked her arms around his neck.

Michael claimed her lips and crushed her to him hungrily.

From a distance, Jennifer heard the sound of waves crashing against the sand and the high-pitched squeal of seagulls diving for fish. Then as her body fused with his, a wondrous joy and certainty flooded her heart, healing old wounds and making her whole again.

"Welcome, home," she heard him whisper.

Indigo Upcoming Release

Cherish the Flame
by
Beverly Clark

Valerie Baker had left her hometown after graduating from college to find a job in her area of expertise in Detroit. She landed a position as an apprentice chemist at Price Industries. She also met and fell in love with Alexander Price, but Michael Price had his own plans for his son's future, and he tries to convince Valerie that she could never fit into Alex's world. When that ploy doesn't work, he uses the information he'd gleaned from the private investigator to finally force her to break it off with Alex and return to her home in Quinneth Falls.

When Alex questions why Valerie has left him, lies are told and secrets are kept. Alex is devastated to learn that the woman he loves has left him. Over the next eight years Alex turns into a wiser, but cynical man making Price Industries his life.

Upon hearing that Valerie was in need and extremely vulnerable, Alex couldn't pass up the chance to step in and bail her out. Now that he had her under his control, he would finally make her atone for her past sins as he saw fit.

Shadows in the Moonlight
by
Jeanne Sumerix

Forest ranger Penny Hart wanted to work where there was more action on the job along with career advancement opportunities. She was excited about the prospect of moving into her parent's cabin and enjoying the solitude of the outdoors. Upon breaking the news to her mother, Penny finds out that her mother has rented the cabin to her deceased father's FBI partner, Mack Holsey.

Undaunted in her quest for greener forests, Penny tells her mother not to worry, that the cabin is big enough for both of them. Of course her mother isn't pleased but goes along with the decision.

On first meeting him, Penny knows Mack is going to be tough to get rid of, which is ultimately her plan. He's warm, comfortable to be with and one heck of a gorgeous man. The two first met five years ago at her father's funeral. Her father had reportedly died in an accidental fall, but her mother and Mack had never accepted that it was just an accident. Thus Mack's reason for returning to Lake Michigan and living in her family's cabin, to uncover the truth.

One night while the two are driving home, they witness a hit and run. A pregnant young black woman dies at the scene. With her dying breath, she asks them to make sure her baby is safe. This is only the beginning of the whirlwind of mysteries and crime the unlikely couple find themselves surrounded by. While Penny and Mack deal with their external strife they are slowly becoming attached to each other. As much as they both fight it... it's there and in a moment of passion they break their promise to themselves and Penny's mother. They had both broken their word and now their feelings for each other were torn between desire and honor.

INDIGO

Winter & Spring 2002

❧ February

Cherish the Flame	Beverly Clark	$8.95
Shadows in the Moonlight	Jeanne Sumerix	$8.95
Indigo After Dark, Vol. IV		$14.95
Dance of Desire	Cassandra Colt	
Skylight Rendezvous	Diana Richeaux	

❧ March

No Apologies	Seressia Glass	$8.95
An Unfinished Love Affair	Barbara Keaton	$8.95

❧ April

Jolie's Surrender	Edwina Martin-Arnold	$8.95
Promises to Keep	Alicia Wiggins	$8.95

❧ May

Magnolia Sunset	Giselle Carmichael	$8.95
Once in a Blue Moon	Dorianne Cole	$9.95

June

Still Waters Run Deep	Leslie Esdaile	$9.95
Everything but Love	Natalie Dunbar	$8.95
Indigo After Dark Vol. V		$14.95
Brown Sugar Diaries part II	Dolores Bundy	

OTHER GENESIS TITLES

A Dangerous Deception	J.M. Jeffries	$8.95
A Dangerous Love	J.M. Jeffries	$8.95
After The Vows (Summer Anthology)	Leslie Esdaile	$10.95
	T.T. Henderson	
	Jacquelin Thomas	
Again My Love	Kayla Perrin	$10.95
A Lighter Shade of Brown	Vicki Andrews	$8.95
All I Ask	Barbara Keaton	$8.95
A Love to Cherish	Beverly Clark	$8.95
Ambrosia	T.T. Henderson	$8.95
And Then Came You	Dorothy Love	$8.95
Best of Friends	Natalie Dunbar	$8.95
Bound by Love	Beverly Clark	$8.95
Breeze	Robin Hampton	$10.95
Cajun Heat	Charlene Berry	$8.95
Careless Whispers	Rochelle Alers	$8.95
Caught in a Trap	Andree Michele	$8.95
Chances	Pamela Leigh Starr	$8.95
Dark Embrace	Crystal Wilson Harris	$8.95
Dark Storm Rising	Chinelu Moore	$10.95
Eve's Prescription	Edwinna Martin Arnold	$8.95
Everlastin' Love	Gay G. Gunn	$8.95
Gentle Yearning	Rochelle Alers	$10.95
Glory of Love	Sinclair LeBeau	$10.95
Illusions	Pamela Leigh Starr	$8.95
Indiscretions	Donna Hill	$8.95

Interlude	Donna Hill	$8.95
Intimate Intentions	Angie Daniels	$8.95
Kiss or Keep	Debra Phillips	$8.95
Love Always	Mildred E. Kelly	$10.95
Love Unveiled	Gloria Green	$10.95
Love's Deception	Charlene Berry	$10.95
Mae's Promise	Melody Walcott	$8.95
Midnight Clear (Anthology)	Leslie Esdaile	$10.95
	Gwynne Forster	
	Carmen Green	
	Monica Jackson	
Midnight Magic	Gwynne Forster	$8.95
Midnight Peril	Vicki Andrews	$10.95
Naked Soul	Gwynne Forster	$8.95
No Regrets	Mildred E. Riley	$8.95
Nowhere to Run	Gay G. Gunn	$10.95
Passion	T.T. Henderson	$10.95
Past Promises	Jahmel West	$8.95
Path of Fire	T.T. Henderson	$8.95
Picture Perfect	Reon Carter	$8.95
Pride & Joi	Gay G. Gunn	$8.95
Quiet Storm	Donna Hill	$10.95
Reckless Surrender	Rochelle Alers	$8.95
Rendezvous with Fate	Jeanne Sumerix	$8.95
Rooms of the Heart	Donna Hill	$8.95
Shades of Desire	Monica White	$8.95
Sin	Crystal Rhodes	$8.95
So Amazing	Sinclair LeBeau	$8.95
Somebody's Someone	Sinclair LeBeau	$8.95

Soul to Soul	Donna Hill	$8.95
Subtle Secrets	Wanda Y. Thomas	$8.95
Sweet Tomorrows	Kimberley White	$8.95
The Price of Love	Sinclair LeBeau	$8.95
The Reluctant Captive	Joyce Jackson	$8.95
The Missing Link	Charlyne Dickerson	$8.95
Truly Inseparable	Wanda Y. Thomas	$8.95
Unconditional Love	Alicia Wiggins	$8.95
Whispers in the Night	Dorothy Love	$8.95
Whispers in the Sand	LaFlorya Gauthier	$10.95
Yesterday is Gone	Beverly Clark	$8.95
Yesterday's Dreams, Tomorrow's Promises	Reon Laudat	$8.95
Your Precious Love	Sinclair LeBeau	$8.95

You may order on-line at www.genesis-press.com, by phone at 1-888-463-4461, or mail the order-form in the back of this book.

Love Spectrum
Romance

Romance across the culture lines

Forbidden Quest	Dar Tomlinson	$10.95
Designer Passion	Dar Tomlinson	$8.95
Fate	Pamela Leigh Starr	$8.95
Against the Wind	Gwynne Forster	$8.95
From The Ashes	Kathleen Suzanne Jeanne Summerix	$8.95
Heartbeat	Stephanie Bedwell-Grime	$8.95
My Buffalo Soldier	Barbara B. K. Reeves	$8.95
Meant to Be	Jeanne Sumerix	$8.95
A Risk of Rain	Dar Tomlinson	$8.95

Indigo After Dark

erotica beyond sensuous

Indigo After Dark Vol. I $10.95
     In Between the Night   Angelique
     Midnight Erotic Fantasies Nia Dixon

Indigo After Dark Vol. II $10.95
     The Forbidden Art of Desire Cole Riley
     Erotic Short Stories   Dolores Bundy

Indigo After Dark Vol. III $10.95
     Impulse   Montana Blue
     Pant   Coco Morena

ORDER FORM

Mail to: Genesis Press, Inc.
315 3rd Avenue North
Columbus, MS 39701

Name _____

Address _____

City/State _____ Zip _____

Telephone _____

Ship to (if different from above)

Name _____

Address _____

City/State _____ Zip _____

Telephone _____

Use this order form, or call 1-888-INDIGO-1	**Total for books** _____
	Shipping and handling:
	  $3 first book, $1 each
	  additional book _____
	Total S & H _____
	Total amount enclosed _____
	MS residents add 7% sales tax